THE FENCING MASTER

Random House / New York

The FENCING MASTER

and Other Stories

GILBERT ROGIN

FIRST PRINTING

 Published in New York by Random House, Inc., and simultaneously in Toronto, Canada, by Random House of Canada Limited.

Library of Congress Catalog Card Number: 65-11288

The stories, "Ernest Observes," "Fielding's Progress," "Judging Keller," "A Description of a Presumption," "Them Apples," "1109 Klingenstein," "At the Sea-Vue Arms," and "Lesser Married" appeared originally in *The New Yorker*. "Chico King, Popular Singer" was first published in *Esquire* Magazine. "A Blessed Day" appeared originally in *Mademoiselle*. "Hello! Goodbye! I Love You!," under the title "Wolf Whistle," and "Anna Banana," under the title "Night Talk," appeared originally in *Vogue*.

MANUFACTURED IN THE UNITED STATES OF AMERICA BY
The Haddon Craftsmen, Scranton, Pa.

Design by Tere LoPrete

To My Mother and Father

Contents

THE FENCING MASTER

Ernest Observes

At the end of summer, along the line that marked the farthest advance of the tide, there lay on the beach the ruin of an enormous fish head. It was, the children told Ernest, the head of a giant tuna. Partially decomposed, battered, consumed, it revealed imperfectly its ingenious interior. The eyes, however, were intact. They stood out desolately, as large as tennis balls—perfect, murky globes that would have made suitable novelties for a czar. At high tide, the head disappeared, withdrawn by the rising water, slipping and tumbling to the dim bottom of the bay. Being preoccupied—writing picture postcards, for example—not once did Ernest notice its submersion nor, since the tide went out at night and again in the morning before he awoke, its emergence. The children, who played all day on the beach—the boy was eight, the girl ten—ignored the head. "Ignored" was not quite accurate, Ernest decided, for that would imply an act of will, suggesting the head was grisly or putrescent and hence something to be avoided. It was, rather, that the head had ceased to be a marvel and held no more interest for them than a grain of sand. They had used it up.

Ernest found the head a compelling and fabulous attraction, and the children's indifference to it disturbed him. He directed their attention to it, indicating its decadent wonders. They listened impatiently, rolling their eyes like players in a silent movie, and replied that prior to this head there had been an even bigger one, which had vanished several days before Ernest arrived and been replaced by the head they now beheld. Ernest didn't know whether to believe them. Perhaps, when the head became commonplace, it no longer appeared as immense as it did when it was first washed ashore. The power of monsters, like the spell of strange summer houses, diminishes with each visit. It seemed unlikely that two great fish heads should land one after the other on this beach. But it might not have been coincidence; the currents might, in fact, be so precise that tuna heads cast off at a certain point and being of certain dimensions would always land at the same place. One would have thought, then, that there would have been a regular succession of heads, since the commercial fishermen must catch a good many large tuna; he imagined a flotilla of fish heads bobbing predictably across the bay. But there was only one, returning daily, ambiguous and implaccable, and each day somewhat the worse for wear, like one's face each morning in the mirror.

In time, Ernest found it wasn't the head itself that engaged him, its obvious splendor and mystery, but the children's attitude to it, to him. He had sought in vain to enlist them as allies in his suit of their mother. He had met her, a divorcée, in the city and followed her to the shore, where a narrow, destitute, shell-strewn garden separated their rented apartments. The children called him, chanting, "old persistent Mr. Ernest McErnest." The head was, in a way, his gift to them, but they already had had one—bigger, and therefore better. This lesser head was the ominous, dwindling emblem of his unsuccess.

Despite his setback with the children, Ernest knew that at bottom he had charm. The many picture postcards addressed to various women testified to this. They all had the same view—the empty, polished, and disquieting interior of a seafood restaurant that bespoke some equivocal disaster in the streets—and they all had, more or less, the same earnest message. The postcards served to appease the infrequent spasms of guilt Ernest suffered from his liaisons. He was conscious of a responsibility to somehow complete his lovers' lives, even if it meant no more than informing them fitfully of his dingy progress. He and they had met on each occasion like two backstrokers colliding head to head, but he felt he had incurred a debt that could not be paid by either an apology or silence.

The incident of the sea snails on Ernest's last day at the shore, while extending the distress brought upon him by the fish head, had more to do, Ernest saw, with his fundamental guilt and, ultimately, with his perpetual failure to make amends or to let go. The children had collected the snails and put them in cans of sea water on the balcony of their apartment. The snails were heaped in the cans as though for sale; Ernest had seen similar shellfish in barrels in Greek markets. Since he never saw the snails move, Ernest did not know whether they were dead or alive. He had considered asking the children, but refrained; it was a cruel question, absurd. After all, what did one feed snails, anyway? The snails' welfare seemed of no concern to the children. When we are young, Ernest reflected, we are hunters. Hunters must not be held accountable; their joy and dominion end with the death or capture of their quarry. They are not judges, nor are they caretakers. If they were, they would not be able to hunt.

The sea water in the cans had gradually evaporated, Ernest observed, and the snails had been forsaken. They might have been hollow shells. Looking at them, Ernest recalled the casualties of his childhood: the baby alligator that had been left one afternoon in the summer sun and had shrivelled up like a mummy; the finches that had never sung in his hearing—at the time, he had had a fantasy that they sang with a thrill and sweetness when no one was home—but only mutely huddled on the trapeze at the top of their cage. The finches had frozen in the winter nights and dropped, one by one, from their perches, the sound of their falls too faint—as light as snow—to awaken him so that he might, perhaps, warm them back to life between his palms. When he found the birds in the morning, not even the radiator could revive them; he flushed them down the toilet. There were, too, the tropical fish he would discover floating on the surface of their tank, horribly rent by one of their number—which one?—in the dark while he slept.

On the afternoon that they were all to leave for the city, Ernest took the cans of snails and dumped them back in the bay. He stood up to his knees in the water and regarded the disorderly heap of snails by his toes. They still gave no sign of life. How light they looked! They had seemed darker when crowded in the cans. He reached underwater and carefully set each one upright. One could move them about like pieces on a chessboard. In the center of every shell, where the spiral design had its origin, was a pale, somehow accusatory eye. Ernest towered above the snails that he had arrayed on the sandy bottom, feeling Olympian, expecting some movement, an acknowledgment of his charity. There was none. Several dozen eyes returned his gaze, and he left unrewarded.

The children were waiting in the apartment, sitting on suitcases like refugees and eating apricots. He felt it was a scene similar to that on the postcards; he had missed yet another disaster. Ernest thought they might have noticed that the snails were gone and ask about them, but they didn't. Their mother was in the kitchen washing the dishes for the last time, putting them in the plastic rack to dry. The dishes would not, Ernest reflected, be used again until next summer. The leap forward in time irritated him. Ernest explored old summers, their mislaid populations, in his mind. He heard, as though from that momentous distance, the children telling him to hurry up and go to his apartment and pack or they would miss the plane. He stared at them for an instant; they appeared to be strangers, chained to the suitcases like monkeys to barrel organs. He told them to pipe down. "I'm just a little boy, but I'm not scared of you, Ernest," said the boy, reasonably. Ernest went out on the balcony. "I'm not scared of you," the boy called through the screen door. Ernest looked down to the spot where he had liberated the snails, wondering if, now that he had gone, they were fanning out, marching silently, vagrantly to sea.

He had often bestowed such small, indifferent gifts of love, interest, and mercy; sometimes he had been rewarded with a sympathetic movement, at other times, as in the case of the snails, with what he considered a reproach. He went heavily into the kitchen. The mother handed him an apricot. He told her about the snails and his disappointment; perhaps if the snails wouldn't pay him back he might at least gain her pity. She told him to eat another apricot, a chocolate pudding, a Frutana; they couldn't take all this stuff back on the plane. He felt, obscurely, that they were all in some kind of peril and were lightening a sinking boat. He was becoming a martyr, Ernest thought—the martyrdom of the snails. Later, as he carried the bags down the stairs, he looked again at the beach. The water was about to reclaim the head. There wasn't enough left of it to stink.

On the flight back to the city, Ernest kept expecting the children to inquire about their snails, to remember that they had left them behind. Children always wanted to take animals home from the country and had to be cleverly dissuaded. Ernest realized that he had prepared a persuasive little speech. But they didn't ask, and he began to feel that their silence was unnatural. Did they know that the snails were dead, that they had, indeed, killed them? Were they feeling the first grip of anxiety? He morosely played Battleship with the boy, who was sitting beside him. He had intended to lose by a narrow margin, but he became aware that he was playing as hard as he could, almost as if his life depended upon his winning. He beat the boy badly, but there was no satisfaction in it; children accept defeat by grownups. Ernest tilted his seat back and announced that he was going to take a nap. The girl told him that was "a big deal." The children hadn't forgotten the snails. They had seen him from the balcony, in his ponderous, clumsy, and pitiable act of self-gratification, and had forgiven him. Was that, Ernest thought, my absolution?

One morning, several weeks later, Ernest awoke in the mother's apartment in the city, where he had spent the night for the first time. She was no longer beside him. He didn't remember her arising; she must have got up to fix the children's breakfast. It was a small apartment—two rooms: the living room, where they had slept on a second-hand Castro, and the children's bedroom, which connected with the kitchenette. Above the boy's bed, attached to the wall with Scotch Tape, was a menu elaborately autographed by Cassius Clay. "Good Luck," it said; Ernest had got it for the boy one rainy morning in San Francisco.

From where he lay, the covers up about his neck,

Ernest could see the children seated at the counter eating cereal out of enamel mugs. Wheat Honeys! Sugar Pops! Corn Kix! He didn't recognize any of the cereals these days. It made him melancholy out of all proportion. Ernest didn't know whether he should pretend to be sleeping. He didn't want to be conspicuous, to embarrass the children. He closed his eyes to slits, as he had done when he was a child, and watched them. From time to time, while he feigned sleep, they got up from the counter and walked past the Castro, in and out of the bathroom—he could hear them demonically brushing their teeth—where the light burned all night to keep the cockroaches in the walls, and then to the table beyond him, looking for their notebooks. He observed, with satisfaction, that notebook covers hadn't changed; they were still darkly marbled, intimating a permanence and a grandeur, like the walls of certain men's rooms.

The children passed him without a glance or a word; they were ignoring him. He opened his eyes wide in protest, turned noisily over and back again. The girl was showing her mother the costume she was going to wear on Halloween. To Ernest it looked like an everyday black dress, but too severe and sombre for a child. "What's *that* supposed to be?" the boy asked. "I'm a mentally ill secretary," the girl said, holding the dress in front of her. Ernest couldn't decide whether she was cute or appalling. He felt at a disadvantage, lying so close to the floor, only his head showing—unshaven and with long, unkempt, graying hair that always seemed more soiled than distinguished. "Why?" Ernest asked. No one paid him the least attention. He felt he was in a kind of juvenile limbo, as though he had been killed in Cops-and-Robbers. "Why?" he pleaded, too loudly. "What am *I* going to be, Ma?" the boy asked. Ernest recalled being awakened in another apartment by a little boy crashing his tricycle into the bed. "Hello, Richard," that benign child had said.

Now their mother was handing them their school lunch. They were at the door in their military berets, leaving. Ernest felt he was watching a film: the actors couldn't respond, stop, turn, explain, go back. He wasn't being ignored, he realized; they were indifferent to him. He had ceased to be a marvel—if, indeed, he had ever been one. He found himself, against his precepts, wondering how the others before him had stacked up—their father. Ernest noticed a great, scarred box, as long as a child's coffin, across the room. It was the toy chest. Lying across it was the necktie he had worn the previous evening. It had been abandoned by another woman's former husband, and Ernest had taken it from her apartment. There had been a bunch of his, the husband's, ties on a hatrack, all tangled up like Medusa's hair.

Ernest rolled over on his back. He felt less oppressed when he could see the full, empty height of the room.

He noticed that the living room was full of, graced with, light. The upper halves of the windows were covered with a translucent Japanese paper in which real autumn leaves were imprisoned, perpetually falling. He didn't know they had maples in Japan—willows, certainly, weeping willows. He imagined Japanese children walking gravely through the woods in a great, silent crowd, at autumn, with burlap sacks over their shoulders, bending down, sorting out the maple leaves, picking them up, and gently stuffing them into their sacks. Somewhere, there were scales, perhaps in a clearing, where a kind, reasonable man—Ernest saw himself in blue Oriental pajamas—weighed the sacks and gave each child a coin. They bobbed in a sort of bow before him, averting their eyes, holding their palms up trustingly. Ernest let his eyes close, shutting out the room. He wished he could be floated free of this exposition of his mutilated age, his anonymity, his furious sorrow, and be sucked back into the shelving declivity of sleep.

Fielding's Progress

Ten years ago, Arthur Fielding's wife held his hand. They had gone for a walk in the ragged hills in back of their hotel on St. Croix and now sat above the pelicans, overlooking the sea. It was their honeymoon. "Vain, selfish, melancholy, and overweight," she said, exploring his palm. Fielding barely feigned listening. In my bureau drawer, he thought, a lizard slumbers in my underwear. In my closet, ants march up and down my neckties. She ticked off his fingers. "Stubborn, stubborn, stubborn," she said. "Dreamer, dreamer." "Um," said Fielding. She let go of his hand.

"What *ever* are you thinking about?" she asked. "Lisbon," he said, vaguely nodding, by way of explanation, toward what he believed, mistakenly, to be the east. She didn't follow his gaze. Instead, she looked at her husband. He has the secret smile of a wife-murderer, she thought.

It was Arthur Fielding's intention that when he left his wife he would visit Lisbon. He had never been there and knew next to nothing about it, but he had laid out an imaginary boulevard in his mind, invested it with time and weather, and, as the years of his marriage went by, inserted its components like a man building a boat inside a bottle. On the boulevard, it was summer, approaching evening, and you could smell the nearby sea. The boulevard was faced with indifferent buildings, formerly residences, which were occupied by a commercial bank, a firm that printed engraved calling cards and letterheads, the offices of an obscure shipping company. In the latter's window, there was a dusty model of an antiquated ocean liner with four vertical funnels. Alongside the ship, completing the display, were two stuffed animals: a hawksbill turtle, whose painted eyes appeared to grieve—for what? —and an inflated blowfish with tattered pectoral fins. Fielding knew that when it grew darker a small bulb would be illuminated within the ship's hull, and the portholes and saloon windows would glow weakly, premonishing disaster. The liner was being menaced by the monstrous turtle and blowfish. Had they already disabled the engine room?

In the center of the boulevard were islands planted with hydrangeas. The flowers were blue, to match the anticipated dusk. Fielding had heard that gardeners buried nails in the ground when they planted hydrangeas, to make the ordinarily pink blossoms turn blue. It was his indulgence that one of the islands was being prepared for planting, the gardeners sowing nails in the spaded earth the way Cadmus sowed the dragon's teeth.

There was little traffic and few pedestrians on the boulevard. One of the few was Fielding. He wore a white linen suit, no longer new, a blue shirt, and a dark-orange tie, and he inhaled, with gratification and desire, the sea and his after-shave lotion. He stood, marooned in his leisure, as though posing for a sidewalk photographer. Indeed, one was coming his way—a young Negro with a religious medal safety-pinned above his heart and a pigeon roosting on his bare head. "Look at the birdie," the Negro said, with a provocative smile. As Fielding looked uneasily into the pigeon's malevolent eyes, the Negro snapped his picture and pressed a soiled card into his palm as if he were passing on plans for an ingenious new naval mine or the address of a beauty salon where dirty movies were shown late at night. Fielding would send the snapshot to his children if it turned out all right.

Although flawed, Arthur Fielding's marriage was, essentially, a success—if you take the view that marriage often resembles a tug of war, in that the husband and wife are antagonists supported by their mutual struggle and if one of them were to let go of the rope the other would fall. Fielding's wife felt she had a right to ask for more than he was willing to give, and while she was trying to forgive him he was waiting for an apology. In the agony of their wordless struggle —the ground rules prohibited either from expressing regret or tormenting the other with the final tyranny of tears—he would hug her warm back, clapped against it in the dark for comfort and security, and out of terror, as an imperilled mountain climber will cling at nightfall to a rock that still retains the warmth of the sun. "What we tell each other about ourselves does not alter who we are," Fielding would say finally, and yearn for an enisling beyond closing a door or turning off a television set, or for the haven he imagined he had had as a child. It was at times like this that he would painstakingly add another element to his fantastic Lisbon. Arthur Fielding dreamed of leaving his wife the way other husbands wistfully dream of catching a blue marlin, hitting a *quiniela exacta*, or taking flying lessons.

The first time Arthur Fielding left his wife, he went to Stuyvesant Town. He had lost his courage on the

Long Island Expressway and told the impartial cab-driver to return to the city when he was still miles from the airport. He stayed overnight, full of apologies and a sense of folly, on the Adamses' living-room couch; Adams and Fielding were architects, who worked for the same firm. Fielding slept badly and awoke screaming "Mommy!" He had heard the great, turbulent wail of an air-raid siren in his dream. It was in fact the Adamses' baby crying. Fielding looked about him with fear and confusion; he had never seen the Adamses' apartment in the morning. For a moment, he thought he was in a glade; there was a dim, greenish cast to the room. Then he recognized the Adamses' flourishing avocado plants on the sill, and next the Adamses, their disembodied faces popping around the doorjamb like Punch and Judy. Fielding refused breakfast and slunk off with his two-suiter, which was adorned with the baggage tags of many airlines, many destinations. His passport, which he had ostentatiously put in the inside pocket of his suit jacket the night before—his wife watching with tolerant derision—jabbed him in the ribs. It had a powerful and surreptitious presence, like a murder weapon. Fielding got a cab, gave the driver his address, which was scarcely a mile across town, and slumped down in the seat. He felt conspicuous, furtive, defeated. He recalled, from an otherwise forgotten classroom, an engraving of Napoleon slouched in a sleigh beneath fur rugs, being hauled back from Moscow to

France in a bad temper. The imploring remnants of his army struggled through the drifts on either side of the road. The artist had tried to make Napoleon's expression sulky and remorseless, but he had always looked to Fielding like a forlorn schnook. I'm a commonplace nut, Fielding thought. He wondered what the cabdriver was thinking about him and sought his face in the rearview mirror.

The next time Arthur Fielding left his wife, he went to Los Angeles. When he had first visited Los Angeles—it had been six or seven years before—he had stayed at the same hotel he was stopping at now. He had arrived then, as now, at twilight, which was his favorite hour, mingling, as it does, longing and regret, promise and speculation. These, Fielding thought, were the dominant notes of his character. On his first visit, he had followed the bellhop, who wheeled his two-suiter on a hand truck, along the winding path that led to his bungalow. In the rear of the hotel, partially enclosed by its wings, there were a number of pink stucco bungalows in a prolific tropical garden. As he looked about him, Fielding saw a naked woman regarding him from a third-floor window. Fielding saw her only for a moment, looking back; he was afraid of falling too far behind the bellhop and losing him in the elaborate, darkening garden. Then, too, as they observed each other, she slowly pulled the drapes across the window. She was in her thirties, Fielding estimated—slender and beautiful. Her skin was unusually rosy, as if she had just got out of her bath, and she was temperately lighted by distant, shaded lamps. Despite her vantage, she did not seem remote or unattainable. Was this the way, Fielding wondered, that princesses held captive in towers appeared to passing princes?

The hotel had apparently changed little in the intervening years. The midget bellboy in the lobby appeared to have grown smaller, or was he a different one? Fielding followed the bellhop through the garden, searching for the woman's window. The palms had surely grown taller, and the window he finally selected as being hers was obscured by their fronds and unlit. Disenchanted, Fielding undressed, took an aimless shower, and got into bed. Before he turned out the light, he stared at the ceiling, discovering melancholy estuaries among its wales and cracks. Later, he had an impulse to call someone up. He rested his hand on the phone in the dark as a king, he imagined, might place a ringed hand upon his orb to reassure himself of his divinity and succession. As he held the receiver, Fielding heard someone typing outside his shuttered windows. He had noticed earlier, in a deep alcove made by the walls of a neighboring bungalow, a sort of open-air office, so dark, recessed, and embowered it might have been Prospero's cell. There someone he took to be a night watchman or maintenance man sat behind a counter. It must be he who was typing so steadily. What was he writing? A report? That wouldn't take him so long. A novel? Awakening once in the middle of the night, Fielding heard the typing continuing.

He arose to the sound of room-service waiters pushing their wheeled tables, the china and cutlery jingling as the wheels crossed the expansion joints in the walks. He had dreamt of a bear that was loose in snowy New York. Hiding in an old apartment building on the upper East Side, he had watched covertly from a window mounted policemen trying to hem it in at a crossing. Behind him he had been aware of vague, solid furniture, dead flowers in a succession of tall, tarnished silver vases, and thick ashtrays of amber-colored glass on metal stands. In one he had seen an ancient cigar butt. The bear suddenly bolted, knocking a horse down. He had later watched the bear being passively led on a leash by a policeman along Madison Avenue. The dream had ended confusedly with his two children dancing for him; a friend's mother, who had been dead a year, wearing a man's double-breasted suit and smoking a pipe; his father shouting.

In the morning, when Fielding opened the door of his bungalow, he smelled the ammoniac odor of the garden. What he smelled was not the fragrant components of the flowers and plants but growth, as in other gardens one smells decay. Nothing was allowed to die here. As soon as a leaf began to yellow or droop, a flower to wither, a gardener snipped it off and took it away.

Sooner than that; the gardeners seemed to anticipate death and worked in advance of it, so they forestalled even age. If a gardener had to step into a flower bed to use his shears, he then swept it clean with a broom, so that the earth never held for long the imprint of the birds or rain. Wasn't it the Eskimos, Fielding asked himself, who put their old people out in the snow, far from the igloos, to die?

Fielding crossed the walk to the outdoor office. Within, barely visible among the shadows and vines, was a man wearing a flashy sports coat. He hardly seemed to be a watchman or to belong to maintenance, but perhaps, Fielding thought, when you went up in that hierarchy this was the way they expected you to dress. But certainly they wouldn't ask someone in the top echelon to sit all day, not even considering all night, in such a damp, exposed place.

"I heard you typing last night," Fielding said.

"Not me," the man said.

"There was someone typing last night," Fielding said. "I'm sure it came from here."

"Did you see him?" the man asked. A breeze moved the vines, and sunlight illuminated his tie for an instant. It was excessively broad and out of fashion, and it was patterned with what looked like giant, warring paramecia.

"No," Fielding said. He now saw a typewriter on the counter.

"Where are you staying?" the man asked.

"Bungalow 11-G," Fielding said.

"Really," the man said. "They don't use that one very often. It must have been the fellow comes on nights you heard. We forget anyone stays there from time to time. I'll talk to him if he's disturbing you."

"He's not disturbing me," Fielding said.

"Oh," the man said. "Yes."

After breakfast, Fielding went to the pool and swam raptly back and forth until he had done a half mile. It was a ritual left over from an earlier religion—one he had practiced as a boy. A woman who was wearing many metal bracelets was in the pool with him. Her bracelets tonkled mournfully underwater and made her sound like an old bell cow. As he swam, Fielding thought he heard himself being repeatedly paged over the public-address system, but when he lifted his head out of the water it was either someone else whom they were summoning or, even more frequently, no one at all, and Fielding pondered the tricks, alarms, and ambiguities of the sea. He recalled swimming once in a clear tropical lagoon and fleeing, panic-stricken, at the approach of an ascending procession of white, globular jellyfish. Much later, he realized, but not entirely with relief, that what they were in fact was great bubbles created by his hands moving through the water. When he had finished swimming, an old, ponderous man lowered himself into the shallow end of the pool as if his body and age were burdens and began vigorously walking in circles, splashing himself with cupped hands and snorting. He told Fielding it was a water-pressure exercise and very salutary. Fielding lay back on a chaise longue and listened to the old man and the Muzak that was piped into the cabañas. He felt uneasy, debilitated, and clumsy. If the world ends violently, Fielding thought, there will still remain the tinny strains of Muzak and great cones, like slag heaps, of rusted razor blades that have been dropped down slots in medicine cabinets.

That evening, his second in Los Angeles, Fielding made up his mind to go out. He was restive, and wanted company; Fielding had learned long ago that what he was truly was a social hermit. But it rained heavily, the hotel driveway was jammed, and the doorman told him it would be hopeless to try to get a cab. He therefore ate alone in one of the hotel's majestic dining rooms. He was the only solitary diner. A strolling trio consisting of a violin, an accordion, and a bass played Strauss waltzes and tunes from "My Fair Lady." The food was wheeled to the tables on carts, where it was warmed over Sterno or theatrically flamed. Fielding noticed the sweating, apprehensive waiters; the windups and flourishes of the captains as they presented a piece of sole or dashed armagnac into a saucepan; asparagus whizzing off plates onto the carpet; Cornish hens bounding under tables; hissed orders and reprimands; reverently kneeling busboys anxiously cleaning up among the diners' feet; the gay, undaunted smile of the bassist as he lugged his instrument between the tables; the purpling faces of the captains, who struggled to maintain an image of innocence in the perilous dining room. It was a scene of agitation and fury, but largely pantomimic. The few words the staff spoke were inaudible in the general roar of dinner conversation and the brave music—Fielding was reminded of the Titanic going down—of the trio. Fielding realized he was the only spectator, the only auditor. The diners were too busy shouting at one another, hitting and missing with their utensils, gobbling as though it were their last meal; the staff was too frantic to be aware of anything save the next swift and chancy movement. He felt he was witness to something that wasn't supposed to be seen, something, in fact, that no one ever saw in its panoramic entirety, like Hell. It became unbearable to attend; it was too charged with the portents of calamity. The dining room appeared to teeter on the brink of a holocaust. Why had *he* been selected to have this backstage view of the dinning, haphazard forces of history? After signing his check, Fielding ran through the rain to his bungalow and lay in bed listening to the soothing and monstrous dripping in the garden.

When Fielding had graduated from college, he went alone on a treacherous pilgrimage to Europe. He recalled now, listening to the rain, imagining it soundlessly joining the Pacific, a room he had stayed in at a second-class hotel in Florence. The hotel fronted on the Piazza Santa Maria Novella, where Fielding had once stood, late at night, watching a votive figure crouched over the trolley tracks in violet light, repairing them with an acetylene torch. The window of Fielding's room looked out on a narrow air shaft. Sometimes, when he awoke there, he thought it was raining—it never was—because there was a bathroom a half flight up the air shaft and the water in the pipes sounded like rain. Two button switches descended from wires down his headboard. One was for the electric light, the other summoned the maid. The first evening he was in Florence, Fielding intended to turn off the light but pushed the wrong button—they were indistinguishable—and then quickly pushed the other as he heard a bell clanging in the corridor like a fire alarm. He lay in panic upon his broad bed, awaiting the maid. When she knocked, he let her in, grinned foolishly in his embarrassment, gestured and shrugged at the two buttons. The maid smiled, said something he couldn't understand, and left. The following night, when Fielding was ready for bed, he started to turn off the light but realized he had forgotten which was the proper button. He looked up at the twisted wires, joined in part by ravelling friction tape, and, rather than take the risk of pushing the wrong button, went to sleep with the light on. In the morning, when he left the room, it was still burning.

When he returned that night, it had been turned off. He undressed in the dark. From then on, he went to sleep in darkness and awoke in darkness. He forced himself, out of self-pity and devotion, to like his room, as a prisoner comes to endure the meanness of his cell for its minor, sour privacy in a life doomed to publicity. He returned to the room at night with affection, to grope for the sink and the towel, to undress and find the bed and sleep. It became his citadel in an alien continent, in a desolate and frightened life. On the ship home, Fielding saw a sea turtle sucked into the screws, presumably to be torn to bits. When he landed, he became engaged to the girl he subsequently married. Fielding often tried to figure out why he had got married. Fear was the most frequent answer. "Fear of what?" he then inquired of himself, and was unable to reply.

The third night that Fielding was in Los Angeles, he took a cab to a bar in Santa Monica. He had been there before on another visit to the Coast; he had designed a high-rise apartment building on Wilshire Boulevard. As he drank, he could smell the dark comforts and covenants of the sea through the screen door. It was as though the screen had strained out the terror of deep places, of monsters with bad eyesight that would suddenly bump into you in their devious cruises. Before closing, Fielding picked up a girl—he later realized that they had picked each other up out of habit, duty, and the gravitation of refugees. He had laboriously related his grievances against his wife and told the girl seriously of his ambition to go to Lisbon and promenade at evening; she had told him about her husband, who had abruptly left her to surf at Sunset Beach in Oahu. She took Fielding home to her apartment in El Segundo in a decrepit Fiat she called "my junk." Her surfboard was lashed above, her sleeping bag rolled up in back. She was a rough-water swimmer, and showed him the gilded trophies on marbled plastic bases she had won. They had a pushup contest, and she defeated him. He had gone first, and then watched her with love and amazement, her plentiful dark hair falling forward, hiding her face, already as anonymous as the faces of the girls of the lawns and lofts of his youth—this strapping creature, her suddenly great, bare arms pushing herself off the terrazzo over and over again, her breathing regular, powerful, and stimulating. She was naked, and her body dazzled with sweat. He sat in his blue oxford undershorts, bewildered and as much in love with this marvel as he had been with the enchanted woman who had once stood at a third-story window and, without a gesture, beckoned to him across the years and miles. Saddened by time's rejections, Fielding told the rough-water swimmer of his all-time personal pushup record—seventy-six—that he had set on the tiled floor of the communal bathroom of the Pensione Robert's in Capri one flushed evening when the island appeared to be so insubstantial it might have been suspended from the swallows that flew above it. Although the accumulated debris of subsequent days and nights had diminished the prominence of this solitary feat, building up about it the way the floor of a rain forest imperceptibly rises with its accretive load over the centuries, it still remained in Fielding's eyes the column that memorialized his progress. Lightheaded and exultant from his exertions on the bathroom floor, its tiles as cold, smooth, and shining as he imagined the surface of a glacier to be, Fielding had felt the floor of Robert's sliding slowly under him, carrying him—an exalted burden!—through the door he had locked in case a passerby had looked in and thought him engaged in some novel perversion, through the corridor that smelled of wet plaster, through the walls and out onto the steep and shadowed slopes of Capri to a distant, predicted, but unknowable moraine. But the flow and impetus, the feeling that he was being borne along by a glacier or, even, on the shoulders of an acclaiming mob, was only, he now realized, the momentum of his descent. He had crested that evening and begun to go downhill.

Fielding awoke in the girl's bed screaming "Mommy!" and found that he was slapping himself on his chest and arms. A number of small insects were rapidly crawling over him.

"What's the matter?" the girl asked, awakened by his desperate movements.

"Bugs," he said, in horror.

"Why don't you kill them?" she asked murmurously.

"I can't," he heard himself saying, with such clarity and understanding that he felt he was about to cry. "They're imaginary."

It happened the year before, too, when he was working on a home in Dallas, the last time he had gone to bed with a stranger. On that occasion, there had been only one insect, large and rather sluggish. A cockroach, he had thought then. His wife had once told him that he could only make love to strangers—fantasy women, that was her phrase. I've got to see a neurologist, Fielding thought. He sat, trembling, on the edge of the bed, trying to get his feet into his shoes. His feet seemed too big, or were his shoes too small? He saw the rough-water swimmer's broad, hard back, surrounded by the tumbled sheets. Innocent and exhausted, she had fallen asleep and was dreaming, Fielding imagined, of the steep waters toward Catalina, of twenty-foot waves at Makaha, of being wiped out in the surf's rubble. What of his wife's dreams and visions? While he had been building his boulevard in Lisbon, had she been furnishing a small apartment in Paris? Fielding called a cab. It had started to become light, a bleak, equivocal false dawn, and the trophies—the bent, golden swimmers poised eternally for dives that would never be completed—gathered glints. When he got up, hearing the cab's horn, and was going to the door, he turned and looked back. It seemed as if the girl were floating on the bed on a dark, undisturbed ocean, being carried softly by the prevailing northeasterlies, those gracious, dependable winds of the southern, summer Pacific, to some protected landfall.

During the long cab ride back to the hotel, Fielding mused about an old Nash he had once owned—the children called it the Gray Ghost—that piece by piece, part by part, had deteriorated around him. The brakes had gone one spring night when they were returning to the city from Peekskill, where his wife's father fed the pigs on his ramshackle farm the sweet stalks of sunflowers. This old man lived a hundred yards apart from his wife, surrounded by cases of raspberry soda; colored postcards depicting Pope Pius XII in profile and views of Italian harbors at sunset were thumbtacked about the clouded mirror that hung above his bureau. On the bureau were tinted studio photographs of his six daughters, and a chased-silver hairbrush that had belonged to his father. It was a relic; the old man hadn't had any hair to brush for years. He had been separated from his wife since the winter of 1935, the result, apparently, of an accumulation of arguments. Neither he nor his wife could recall any longer what they had argued about so long ago. Instead, they evolved, over the years, a great lore of mythic, rather melodramatic differences that seemed to suit their purposes and to set them free from any lingering regrets. In the safety of his kitchen the old man would pound on the oilcloth-covered table and say that his wife had been telling people that he had wept when she suggested he sell his pigs, which, she often noted, were depreciating and stinking up the property. "Grandma getting old," he would declaim, and wink so as to include Fielding in his cunning and conspiracy. He generally had dinner in her kitchen every evening, however, bearing before him as he approached, like a lantern in the storm, a bottle of raspberry soda. From where Grandma waited on her porch, screened by her climbing geraniums, she could see the soda irradiated by the light of the setting sun that passed through the bottle. In the winter, the soda cast its color on the snow. It was, Fielding thought, as though the old man had, in a moment of absent passion, blown on his heart like a coal.

The evening the brakes failed, Jimmy, Fielding's son, had wanted to take home from Peekskill a little pig he had named Pinky Puddles. Fielding had told him, in the patient, statesmanlike voice he reserved for such occasions, that it was against the law to keep little pigs—or, for that matter, big pigs—in the city, and Jimmy had cried. A few miles from Peekskill, Pinky Puddles was forgotten and Jimmy and his sister, Emily, were singing rounds in the back seat of the car: " 'Heigh-ho, nobody at home. Drink nor meat nor money have I none.' " It had seemed to Fielding that the road to the city was downhill all the way, and he had rushed along it in the dark feeling both dread and exhilaration, without slackening speed or shifting gears. The scent of honeysuckle that entered, almost palpably, the open windows, and the sweet, artless voices of his children, cast a benevolent spell about them all, until the Nash came to a miraculous, providential halt in front of their building.

On Sunday nights in the summer, Fielding would drop his wife and children off at their door and circle restlessly, vagrantly the silent, empty blocks, searching for a parking place. Sometimes it would take him as much as an hour before he found one, and he would become lulled by his slow, circular investigation. In his fatigue, he imagined he was in an eccentric orbit, being carried farther and farther away in increasingly vast circles, growing old and forgetful, at times losing his original, ancient purpose, at others recalling, paroxysmally, his wife waiting in front of the "Late Late Show," the pure faces of his children asleep in the diminished, distant apartment. When he finally found a space, he'd slump over the worn wheel, dizzy and depleted from his quest and the effort of parking, and listen to the small, expiring clicks and wheezes of the cooling engine—noises, he thought, that a beetle might make in the grass if you lay down and listened, ear up against shard, to its meticulous progress. Then the depressing miracle would occur. He would hear the steady ticking of the car clock. It was only on these occasions that he was reminded that it worked—one of the few bits of machinery in the Nash that still did, ticking away with some improbable time on its face, as though it had only a casual connection with the disintegrating car. Fielding was not altogether sure that the clock ran all the time—it couldn't, as he only became aware of it at these late, mysterious hours. The functioning clock filled Fielding with anger and remorse; its perseverence was so pointless, wrong-headed. The Nash was a hopeless cause. It wasn't fair. It was a reproach; he saw in it what he had seen long ago in the eyes of animals—woodchucks in upland pastures—that he had intended to kill but only wounded.

When Fielding returned to his bungalow, he lay rigidly in bed, waiting for sleep, as though it was an irresistible adversary with whom he was expected to wrestle and always lost. After a while, he heard the typing. It, like the clock, must have been, couldn't have been, going on all the time. The fellow typed on and on, furiously, pausing only, it seemed, to insert a new page. I know what the bastard's typing, Fielding suddenly realized, inspired. The bastard's typing the story of my life.

Arthur Fielding waited until exactly eight on the fourth evening he was in Los Angeles before calling his wife. It would be 11 P.M. in New York and she would be watching John K. M. McCaffery; the children would be sleeping. Their telephone rang many times.

"Hell-o."

Fielding heard the sullen, uncommitted syllables of one of his two children. For some reason, he thought, children develop a special telephone voice. It is neutral, and more awed than apprehensive, as if they expected some challenging authority to be on the other end of the line—their principal or a white-bearded God whimsically awarding gold stars from his throne.

"Hello," Fielding said.

"Art-bo," the child said.

"Jesus Christ," Fielding said under his breath.

"You'll have to speak up, old boy," the child said.

Fielding could never tell Jimmy from Emily at first.

"Where are you calling from, Art-bo?"

"Los Angeles."

"Working on a house?"

She hadn't explained his absence. Right? Wrong? What would he have done? "Yes," Fielding said. Why not, for now?

"That's logical," the child said. "It's a bit chilly in New York, with a slight breeze. Did you know, Art-bo, that birds go south in the autumn and come north in the spring? We learned that at school today. I saw one."

"One what?" Was it Jimmy?

"One going south."

"Where's Ma?" Fielding asked.

"In the medicine cabinet."

It was Jimmy. That was one of his secret phrases. He would never say where he picked them up or what they meant. Fielding reflected that children have many more secrets than adults do, and keep them, often, forever. No, they lose them when they grow up, not giving them away but forgetting them. What secrets had Fielding mislaid? That one night, through a pair of mother-of-pearl opera glasses with which his mother had once watched Elsie Ferguson and Alice Brady, he had spied on a naked lady carefully making her bed across the street? She was wearing glasses and had made, he recalled, hospital corners. He crouched, trembling, in the farthest, darkest corner of his room, as though cornered by his guilt. At moments, as he peered through the opera glasses, his eyes watering, her image becoming unfocussed, it had appeared as though the lady were looking at *him*, with amusement and some scorn. Once, when she disappeared from his field of vision, he imagined that she had gone to the phone to call up his parents, and he waited in dread for the phone to ring, the footfalls as his parents came down the corridor in their robes. At the next opportunity, which was a few nights later, he looked for her, but her windows were dark. The following morning, he saw that her apartment was empty, the familiar bed gone. The floor was lighter where it had stood. She must have moved away, and he felt cheated and bereft.

"Jimmy, where the hell is she?" Fielding said.

"Don't get flustered," Jimmy said. "In the Adagio, I told you."

The Adagio was a neighborhood bar that she had taken him to on one of their first dates. Although they went there often, he could never get accumstomed to the name. Affettuoso; why not the Affettuoso? At times when, for one reason or another, he had failed to make love to his wife when she expected him to, she would get up, dress, and go down to the Adagio. It had preceded him. It was her home base. She felt safe there. From what? Did he menace her with his indifference? With his egoistic, self-commiserating, tiresome search? He saw, in a fresh moment of horror, the blowfish, the allusive threat of the gay photographer. The hydrangeas had wilted and looked like old foam on a beach; it had been a dry, barren summer in Lisbon. Why was he so grave and cautious, bending enough to believe but never enough to be carried away? She would return from the Adagio while he was sleeping, and in the morning they would look at each other accusingly across the debris of the breakfast table. The fire hadn't gone out. It was banked, banked against some long, unexpected, and improbable winter.

"What's she doing there?" he asked, hoping wildly for an appeasing, miraculous answer. What?

"She's on the bottle," Jimmy said.

"Stop horsing around, kid," Fielding said.

"Give 'em hell, Art-bo" the boy said.

"Jesus Christ," Fielding said.

"Don't swear in front of us kids."

"What you been doing, Jimmy?" Fielding asked.

"We were up at Grandma's. She told Ma I should be baptized."

"What did Ma say?"

She told Grandma to take me downtown and get me baptized if it made her happy. Emily's saving her allowance to buy a Bible. I think we should all go to church every Sunday and confess."

"Confess?" said Fielding.

Heigh-ho, nobody at home. He couldn't get it out of his head. Confess. What ever happened to Pinky Puddles? Why wasn't she at home when that was where she was supposed to be?

"Emily and me played with rocks," Jimmy said. "And Grandpa let us build things out of wood. Let's move to the country. It's awful in New York. Everywhere you look there's a big thing in front of you. There's a big thing this way and a big thing that way. You're surrounded."

"Where's Emily?" Fielding asked wearily.

"She's sleeping."

"Is Ma really in the Adagio?"

"I told you. I got the number in case there's a forest fire or a tidal wave or something."

"Oh."

"I forgot to take my pill," Jimmy said.

"Your pill?"

"My little lover pill."

"What?"

"Dr. Wacky's Little Lover Pills for Promotion of Love Bug Bites. Do you want to hear the ingredients? Sugar, licorice, gum arabic, flour, artificial color and flavoring, net weight."

"Yes," Fielding said.

"I got to go back to sleep now, Art-bo, so I can watch more birds go south tomorrow. Whyn't you come home and build a middle-income project, so you can look with me? Ma loaned me Grandma Fielding's pearly binoculars. You can see everything up close."

"Yes," said Fielding.

"Bye, Daddy."

Fielding looked in the phone book, then dialled a number.

"American Airlines. Reservations. Miss Endicott speaking. May I help you?"

Dark hair? Wearing one of those white blouses that button in the back. You can see the brassière through it.

". . . help," Fielding repeated, tonelessly.

Judging Keller

Keller writes in his notebook, "I am sitting on a dunce's stool at the kitchen counter, being defeated in war by my son, who keeps dropping the cards on the floor. If it is a game of luck, why do I always lose? My daughter is in her room. I can hear her playing a popular love song on the Hum-A-Zoo I bought her at the Feast of St. Anthony, a street fair. She is not playing for me but for Barbie and Ken and Barbie's best friend, Midge, the dolls that are advertised on television. My son tells me, with a wonder I have mislaid, that it is snowing out."

. . .

In fact, Keller is sitting beneath an awning in a launch. There are three launches drifting as one in the lagoon of the atoll; they are held together by hands on the gunwales. In the boat with Keller is a child who he believes is dying of meningitis. With her are her parents, her brothers and sisters, and a group of friends and relations. The two other launches are similarly loaded. Everyone is waiting for the flying boat that will take the girl to the hospital. In respect for the occasion, the natives are dressed as though they were going to church. The men are wearing shirts, and several have woollen sports jackets on, too, despite the heat; the woman wear dresses printed with flowers they have never seen. Keller has gathered that someone must have radioed for the plane, as it normally comes only on Thursdays and Sundays and today, he is quite sure, is Saturday. Keller is not at all clear about what is going on; he does not speak either French or Polynesian. For instance, they still think he is a doctor.

Keller's incertitude began, in one sense, when he examined the hydrographic chart of the archipelago before arriving at the atoll three days ago. In another sense, indecision, bafflement, and unease had been Keller's company for some years. The chart was full of cautionary and foreboding notations. Stirred by these disquieting auguries, Keller made a list of them:

The geographic positions are approximate.
The north point lies 3 miles further west.
Reported to be 2 miles closer than charted.
Soundings in fathoms reduced to approximately Lowest Low Water.
The lights are reported to be unreliable.
Disappeared 1938.
Very strong currents.
Remarkable gap.
Dangerous.

He felt, besides, that if someone had sounded and surveyed *him* he would, no doubt, have published just such indeterminate and apprehensive findings. But then, weren't they always fumbling over him with a plumb line and transit? Why was he so frequently assailed and indicted by moralistic cabdrivers and unrepentant relief doormen, reproached by the sullen glances of subway change clerks? Not long ago, a cabdriver had told him, full of condescending sorrow, that he, Keller . . . Well, he had said, after Keller had criticized him for missing a light, "Mister, you're a mean man." Then he had explained that at sixty-seven he was twice Keller's age, that his reactions were no longer as quick as Keller's, and that he had, only the other day, buried his wife of forty-three years. Keller would never forgive him for the last, gratuitous blow. What right had that anonymous old man in a madras cap—no doubt he was wearing matching Bermuda shorts as well—to involve him in his anguish? He *buried* her! *That* was an achievement! Had he shovelled the clods in with his own hands? A final presumption.

Shortly after that judgment, Keller had been confronted by Mr. Gallagher. Mr. Gallagher had owned a laundry called Mrs. Gallagher's French Hand Laundry & Dry Cleaning. From time to time, Mr. Gallagher would post a sign in the window announcing that the laundry was moving to a new and larger location, but the new store was always darker, more cramped, and meaner than the old one. Keller often found occasion, in one store or another, to reprove Mr. Gallagher—buttons were missing or broken, a shirt was torn or had phenomenally shrunk. Mr. Gallagher would tell him, with wrath, righteousness, and fatigue mixed in his rasping voice, that the laundry business was not what it once was, that help these days was indifferent and clumsy and demanded not only higher wages but hospitalization—and, at last, that he, Mr. Gallagher, would make it up to him. Mr. Gallagher would then punch the "No Sale" key on his rickety cash register as though he were detonating a charge that would mercifully blow him to bits. The cash drawer was generally empty, so Mr. Gallagher would next grub in his pockets—he wore, like a scarecrow, ill-fitting and unlikely garments abandoned by customers—until he came up with, besides the tatters and rubble of ancient Kleenexes, a few soiled bills that he would tediously smooth out. At least he didn't tell Keller what had happened to Mrs. Gallagher.

Exhausted and unnerved by this ritual, Keller surreptitiously switched to a Chinese laundry. One day, walking by Mr. Gallagher's latest store, he noticed that it was empty and that there was a "For Rent" sign in the window instead of the usual doomed prophecy. A few weeks later, Keller came home on a Monday night and found a new relief doorman sitting on a bench in the lobby. He was wearing a uniform that was much too small for him, and he had drawn his visored hat over his eyes as though he were ashamed to admit his identity. His feet, however, were thrust contemptuously forward, revealing white cotton socks and extraordinarily pale, venous legs expressive of age and hard times. The doorman was, of course, Mr. Gallagher. He did not get up or greet Keller as Keller walked to the elevator, only stared at him with disdain, anger, and ponderous suffering before turning away. Keller ascended, assailed by rage and guilt, hardly relieved by the thought that he would not have to face Mr. Gallagher until the following Sunday. No, this man hiding bitterly in the shadow of a borrowed hat had been pulled down so harshly by circumstance that he had been stripped even of "Mr." and of "Gallagher." Now he had only a first name—Keller wondered what it would turn out to be—like, say, a draft horse.

But their next encounter never came about; several days later, Keller was flying toward the South Pacific, encumbered, as he often was on planes—was it a factor of altitude?—with sentimental wellings and constrictions. He smelled strange soaps and toilet waters on his hands and tenderly inspected them. What had he been doing last night, stumbling up and down the withered hills among the eucalyptus that emitted the odor of urine, of fear and childhood, amorously holding a sleeping child in his arms? On his stopover in Los Angeles, he had taken out this little girl's mother. They had left the child at a neighbor's, and afterward he was carrying her in the dark to her bedroom, where a dusky cat sat on the sill; he remembered climbing the stairs, frightened that he would drop her—he was really very drunk and she had become terribly heavy—or that her lolling head would hit the banister. As he climbed, he thought, at the same time aware of his pretension, of Abraham burdened and tormented by Isaac. Was the soap, then, the child, the toilet water the mother? Their sweet, confiding traces consoled him. He wished he could be mapped at that benevolent moment. He would even lay back his skin and tissue and expose the soft machinery, each organ brightly and childishly colored like the different countries on a tin globe.

Keller writes in his notebook, "I am sitting against the wall in the smoking section of the Leroy Street pool, facing the sun. I would be no more dazed and acquiescent if a firing squad should march casually out of the men's locker room and, turning, confront me. I gather I have done something wrong—or not done something, an act of neglect that was just as much a fundamental crime or error—and eventually I am to be punished. I have been callous and lofty; self-righteous, too, I suppose. I cannot confess, either to commissions or omissions, for I am not sure what it is they expect of me. But I am so agitated when faced with only the *possibility* that I have offended that I simply accept my doom and give up. I know I exaggerate, but in this mood the water in the pool seems as viscid and murky as that in which hippopotamuses might lurk, where stones knocked together underwater would not be heard. One hippopotamus, two hippopatamus, three hippopotamus. Several kids are playing a game in front of me. They have dropped a book of matches—the cover advertises the Valley of the Estancia Ranchettes—on the concrete and are trying, without success, to spit on it. My left arm is about my son, my right arm is about my daughter. When they judge me with rifles, they will have to judge us all. But, for the moment, we are talking intimately, conspirators three, about our new apartment.

"My daughter says, 'My room is going to have either pink or lemon-yellow walls, depending on whether I get a pink-and-white or yellow-and-white canopy bed. The yellow has to be lemon yellow, but the pink can be just pink. I think I'd rather have it lemon yellow and with curtains that come all the way down to the floor. It's going to be my house on rainy days and my brother can't make it dirty. If I let him inside, he has to clean his feet first.'

"My son says, 'I'm getting awfully sick of the word "lemon yellow." '

"I want to say, 'Can I hide in there with you?'

"My son says, 'In *my* room I want a little modern desk and a little modern typewriter, one little toy cupboard—because I'm going to give most of my toys away to little kids—one medium-sized window and my light, my little light, my light.' "

Keller looks about him at the ring of dark, committed faces. Oppressed by their trust and reverence, he takes the child's wrist. Her pulse is faint and rapid. He lays his head upon her chest as though he were lowering a great, unwanted weight, and wishes he could reside, obscurely penitent, on that hard, hot, ribbed casket. The flutter of her heart intrudes and he looks at his watch. Her pulse must be two hundred. He sits up and futilely examines the empty sky. The others obediently follow his gaze. The girl cries out. What was it they called it in "Introduction to Neurological Medicine"? The hydrocephalic cry? Now the rest are watching him again. Simon says write in your notebook or you will lose your mind. Keller feels the intolerable burden of his upper lip upon his lower.

Keller did not like islands, but he was drawn passionately to them the way the salmon is tugged upstream. He had once met a penniless alcoholic who had drifted infallibly from San Francisco to Miami one summer, vaguely searching for an ex-wife. This man could not have told you the purpose of his pilgrimage; the ex-wife was the same sort of perhaps sentimental goal as a grave is, or a mountaintop. As it turned out, by the time he got to Miami his ex-wife was in Ohio, but he found instead, as though he had spied it from afar and it had been his target all along, a half bottle of Marie-Brizard crème de menthe hidden behind a giant box of Tide in the cupboard beneath the kitchenette sink. He finished it, replaced the empty bottle in a flourish of guilt, and presumably returned, without solace, to San Francisco. Another time, in the same vein, Keller had crossed paths with an elderly Chinese. He had seen this solitary three times in as many months, pausing, in pensive regard, hands clasped behind him, bent slightly forward as though at a high window: in Geneva, before a bed of plants growing in the image of a swan; considering flounders and soles in an aquarium in Göteborg; in Rome, scrutinizing a statue of a hermaphrodite. Keller imagined that the Chinese was undertaking a vast and penitential journey.

Behind him, in the distance, there was death in a hall bedroom, disorder in the kitchen garden.

The more remote and the smaller the island was, the more desperately Keller sought it out; once it was achieved, he settled into melancholy and desolation, tranced by the imposition of his austerities. He was an admirer of St. Simeon Stylites, who dwelt on higher and higher pillars. Many years ago, Keller had observed in a restaurant a large, grave, and somehow ecclesiastical trout that maintained itself by cursory strokes of its fins in the exact center of a fish tank. The tank was too small to permit the trout to advance or retreat more than an inch, or to turn around—and, of course its destiny was assured and imminent, and Keller envied it its equilibrium.

On this occasion, Keller was visiting the most populous of the islets that, configured like a jawbone, made up the atoll. In the afternoon, he would walk through the coconut palms to the bleak esplanade of the reef and moon about it in his tennis shoes, at times stooping to examine a sea urchin or a turbinate shell, at others gazing sententiously at the Pacific. He would often speculate about the intricate foundations upon which he was standing. He understood that the reef was a great mausoleum composed of the skeletons of innumerable animals, but he wondered whether the coral was still silently dying beneath his feet, whether he was, at this moment, precariously balanced and uplifted by rapid generations.

Death and its relics, though they were less monumental and ingenious than the coral reef, seemed to be impinging upon Keller in recent months. While packing for this trip, for instance, he had come across an artificial pink egret plume that had been hidden under some shirts that still bore the mark, or stigma, of Mrs. Gallagher's French Hand Laundry. The plume came from the scanty costume of a French dancer; it had fallen, too light and gaudy to be a presentiment, into Keller's lap during a lounge show in Las Vegas and he had saved it. He had later read that the dancer had asphyxiated both herself and her toy poodle—also dyed pink, the paper reported—in her efficiency unit in the Paradise Valley Apartments. The plume retained, years afterward, the not wholly agreeable odor of her makeup.

There were, too, Sylvia's letters, which he kept in a shoebox, along with old Christmas cards, on an all but unattainable shelf at the top of his hall closet. Sylvia had, over the years, glanced across Keller's life like a stone shied across water, but it was only when she sank—in reality, leaping from a hotel window in, of all places, Baltimore—that she became lodged in his consciousness. The last time he saw her, he was standing on a dim platform in Pennsylvania Station; they had just said goodbye. Looking through the window of the parlor car Miles Standish, he had watched her revolving gravely in her chair. He waved, but she was turning faster and faster, as though on a carrousel, and apparently did not notice him.

One day, Keller took the letters down and read them over, copying passages in his notebook that underscored his irreparable failure and default.

> I have been thinking [she had written] that I'll take your abominable overcoat to the cleaners, so that you'll look more like the sterling young man you are when you get back. Would you please send me a valentine. Since fifth grade I have never gotten one except from Ginger [Sylvia's daughter] and she usually makes me make the one she sends me. Ginger says she would like to work in your office because she likes your sliding door, also the music in the elevator. Thus is youth moulded. (Brit. sp.) . . .
>
> Last night sitting under an arctic moon and eating bean soup, I thought of you. Aren't you the lucky boy to inspire such, ah, er, I can't think of the right word, but something like a religious fervor springing from base carnality. I have managed to fake the morning away and, lo, it is time for lunch. But my mid-morning jelly doughnut lies heavy on my heart, so maybe I'll just walk. Today spring seems to have come to New York. I have an overpowering urge to buy a hyacinth. . . .

My social life has been proscribed by a variety of circumstances that are nauseating to me. I can't do anything with Mitchell because he might try to break another coffee table with my head and/or he is violently on the make, a combination of danger and flattery that I'd rather watch on TV. Henry Lansdorf is not only a fink but absolutely rotten right down to the worm at the core of his being, besides being a pothead and a lush, among other things. I don't like him very much, either. I went to a party last night. A man who is probably an assistant buyer told really dirty, non-funny jokes. The walls were covered with burlap, which makes me sneeze, and I was introduced to a man who once painted a portrait of the Pope and owns all the postcard rights. Diana went to the opening of the new El Morocco. Some of the waiters are Pinkerton men, she thinks. I wish I had somebody to talk to. . . .

Yesterday I washed your telephone and vacuumed your lampshade. Agnes [Keller's maid] says you are out of Mr. Clean. The only mail was from your Daitch Shopwell. Kel, I miss you. . . .

Olivio, the man who feels his own paintings, called just now. "How's your aesthetic boy friend?" he asked. It made me visualize you, chiaroscuro on a beach. Send me a swatch of your skin so I can see how brown you are. I will send you a plastic giraffe filled with bubble bath that is in the window of the Commodore drugstore. I had a long look at myself in a triple mirror the other day and decided that if I don't do something I will soon look like M. Pneu. I think I am going to a track meet. What does one wear? I have never been to a track meet. . . .

Tell me a joke please, a funny one. . . .

There was another letter, the contents of which he could hardly recall, which he had not copied out passages from, and which stirred him like the strong movements and sentiments of a forgotten dream. It was not a letter in the strict sense, having never been sent. Sylvia had typed it in Keller's apartment; she had gone there on a winter afternoon to water his philodendron. He found it when he returned from one island or another with plastic sandwich bags full of shells. He was not certain where the letter was now. After Sylvia killed herself, he mailed it to a mutual friend; it described scenes of her childhood, something about an immense tree that she climbed and hid in, inconspicuous and vulnerable. The tone was both morose and mocking, and Keller felt that in some fashion the letter expiated him; that is why he forwarded it. At the time, this friend was living in Arkansas, in the Ozarks. He wrote back about the tarantula that had its hole in one of the earthen steps that led to the spring, and the soft-shelled turtles that his neighbor killed; he cut off their heads and hung the turtles upside down from boughs along the stream to drain. It was then spring. Sylvia was not mentioned. Months later, Keller got a postcard from a motel in Chihuahua; the friend was pushing south. Keller thought of him walking in the desert, heavy with reproof, Sylvia's letter crumpled in his pocket like one of Mr. Gallagher's dollar bills.

Sylvia asked Keller to marry her while they were driving to Key West in an air-conditioned Hertz car with tinted windows which he had rented in Miami. He told her—if he could no longer remember what she said without looking at his notes, or even what she looked like, except that she had a brilliant nose like Petrarch's, he could still hear his own dreadful, commonplace sentence; it groaned in his ear like the artificial ocean in the conch with "Greetings from Key West, Fla." painted upon it which Sylvia bought for her daughter—"It's not that I don't want to marry you, Sylvia; it's only that I just don't want to get married now." She moved away from him and stared out through the windshield at the dark, stormy colors of the sea and roadside; the cold, continuous rush of air blew between them; they might have been standing on a platform between railway coaches passing through the Alps. Instead of turning back, they continued to Key West—a shabby dénouement. In the afternoon, they swam in their motel pool; the water was as hot as blood and filmed with suntan lotion. In the evening, they ate in a seafood restaurant that had comically illustrated maps of Key West as placemats. Sylvia kept going to the ladies' room to cry; "Mermaids" was written on the door. That night, they lay under a bas-relief: two snowy egrets and several stalks of bamboo beaten out of copper. She gripped him and implored him to marry her, and he heard himself, carefully selecting his words. . . . Many years before, Keller had walked barefoot to the end of the rocky mole that extends into the Adriatic at Venice. It was an unreasonable undertaking, but this lack of purpose or profit was, in a way, its justification. Without actually doping it out in these words, Keller wanted to see—and not very badly, at that—what it was like at the end, although he knew from experience that it would not be dissimilar to the beginning or the middle; all he would find there was the way back. It was July; Italy was suffering a heat wave; the rocks were hot, and their fragments cut into his bare soles. But Keller's discomfort was alleviated by the fact that with each step he was getting closer to his indifferent goal—the light and the fishermen, who had rowed out, sitting about it. The return, however, was entirely an ordeal. It was a reversion, and every step carried him nearer to a place that he had been to, and back to attitudes, briefly suspended, that brought him no comfort. Now, as he spoke to Sylvia, fair-minded and conciliatory, he felt he was picking his way slowly back along the rocks, searching for a smooth foothold, putting his foot down gingerly in the expectation of pain, at turns grieving, bored, and philosophical, the shore appallingly distant.

There was a radio in the wall of the motel room which could not be turned off. Faint, tinny, and incomprehensible voices seeped out of the grille. A man in the room next door was singing "Lady of Spain." As she held him, Sylvia trembled so that he disengaged her arms and legs, got out of bed, and turned the air-conditioner down to "L," for "Low."

When they returned to New York, Keller continued to see Sylvia on and off out of a sense of guilt and pity and, rarely, desire. He knew he was being irresponsible; he had wantonly led her out and now, instead of abandoning her, he was dragging her back. She asked him to marry her several more times, they had tearful scenes, and, finally, she took the train to Baltimore. She said she was going to visit an aunt. When she died, Keller owed her nine dollars. He thought of cancelling the debt by buying a present for her daughter, who was living with her grandparents in Cedarhurst, but he was not sure whether it would be in good taste, and in time he forgot the particulars of his obligation. Keller came to blame himself for Sylvia's death, a position that was not without an element of self-gratification; it gave him, like the fur and skeleton of the slain mouse in the owl's crop, a substantive ache about which he could wind and justify his doubt and discontent. The owl shortly coats and eliminates this sharp, indigestible relic, but Keller preserved his memory of Sylvia as though, in a secret and uncharted crypt, she and his shameful forebear, the sterling young man, lay side by side.

On his third morning on the reef, Keller heard someone shouting and, looking up, saw a young man in a red *pareu* jogging toward him. He beckoned to Keller and shouted again, "Kel-lair!" For a moment, Keller thought he had run all the way from the village to ask the time. Keller watched him approach with disbelief; he had come to regard the reef as his garden. If he had a garden, Keller thought, it would be like this—bitter and weedy. The intruder tugged at Keller's arm. "Kel-lair," he repeated in an almost sweet, despairing voice, and Keller realized, with wonder and relief, that he was saying his name, and what he wanted was Keller to return with him to the village. As though he felt the draw and agency of fate, Keller submissively followed. To keep up, he had to run. The native led him to a house shaded by breadfruit trees. It seemed to Keller that the entire population of the village was squatting on the front lawn. What had *he* done? Or what was he about to do, more like it. Or was it doomsday or a revolution? The young man took him by the hand and drew him through the silent and ambiguous crowd. Keller stooped as he entered the house, although the doorway was high enough; he felt extradorinarily tall and condemned to make unnecessary adjustments. Curtains hanging from fishing line divided the interior into a series of cubicles and blocked the light. The windows must have been open, for every so often the curtains, which were unevenly drawn, giving the effect of an elaborate maze, billowed theatrically. Keller was led this way and that, baffled and apprehensive. Once, he blundered into a chicken; it plunged into a curtain as though beheaded. At times, he lost sight of his guide as he preceded him around corners; the only sign of his presence was the pressure of his hand. At times, too, a curtain would abruptly part, someone would stare at Keller without expression and then would pull the curtain to. At last, the guide stopped and stepped aside. Before Keller was his reward, a girl of five or six lying on a bed as high as an altar. She was breathing rapidly and held her head in an odd, stiff position. Keller laid his hand on her forehead; she was burning up. He tried to move her head, and she screamed. Appalled and intimidated, Keller stepped back and found his way obstructed by people who had followed him in and stood behind him on tiptoe. He now noticed that there were others crouching on the floor about the bed.

"I'm not a doctor," Keller said fatuously.

There was no reply.

"You don't understand," he pleaded. "I'm sorry, but

you're mistaken. I'm really not a doctor. What do you want of me?"

As though in response, a chair was brought to the head of the bed and Keller was gently pushed into it. He did not want to look at the child, but neither could he look at the supplicant and reliant faces of those who surrounded him. They, not she, were to be his clement nemeses. They must have discovered somehow that he had once gone to medical school. Were there clues or ruins in his face, manner, and belongings—the spoor of old declinations? Was it true that hunters could tell by the depth and temperature of the pool of urine how large an elephant had passed how long ago? But did they know, further, that he had left medical school because (he told himself, no doubt falsely) he was unable to endure the pain of strangers—that vast, abstract, public suffering and, more to the point, the infinite and irrational trust? He could not just sit there, eyes cast down, however, for the little girl had begun to twitch spasmodically; he could feel it through his knee, which was inadvertently touching the bed. He yearned to be elevated like St. Simeon Stylites, who was finally sixty feet tall, governing and forgiving by sighs. Perhaps, he thought, if she died here and now he could say—but who would listen?—they came for him too late. No, she was moaning. Keller was fairly trapped. He leaned forward and carefully bent the child's neck. Her legs flexed in response. He pushed one of her thighs against her abdomen, then extended it. She cried out—a cry high-pitched and piteous like that of birds that follow a ship far at sea—and her other leg flexed quickly while the one he held strained against his hand. The signs of Kernig and Brudzinski. She had the classical symptoms of acute meningitis, the lecturer would say, lifting his voice in that high, dingy hall that seemed a place of departures, like a railway terminal. "Hallucinations, delirious states, maniacal episodes, and restlessness." He called them out as though they were stations down the line. Who were Kernig and Brudzinski anyway? Keller pictured them standing on a snowy corner by the great, dark loom of a hospital near the North Sea, waiting for the last bus. They were identically dressed in long overcoats with fur collars upon which the snow did not melt but built up about their dispassionate faces. Keller forced himself to take the child's pulse. It was a hundred and eighty.

"We've got to get her to the hospital," he announced. Why were all his sentences so banal? It's not that I don't want to marry you, Sylvia. . . . He could have said that, for all they knew, for all that it mattered.

Keller took out his notebook and drew, without perspective, a building with many windows and a cross on it, then a seaplane; a dotted line ending in an arrow connected them. He felt like adding a chimney and a coil of smoke, Kernig and Brudzinski waiting for the bus. He tore out the page and they passed it among them. When it was handed to the last, who was the young man they had sent to bring him here, he nodded and left. The others made lifting motions with their arms. What did they want of him now? Or was it a dance? But celebrating what—or carry her where? He bent and picked her up, and all the curtains suddenly shot back and Keller saw that he was only a few feet from the door. The crowd on the lawn rose as he stepped out and parted with ceremony to allow him to pass. Some went before on the road, and he followed them; looking back, he saw the rest bringing up the rear, joined now by the village's abused and crippled dogs. He felt like a prisoner under escort. They were walking by the harbor. He recalled carrying that other sleeping child through the fragrant and treacherous hills. How many nights ago? Abraham and Isaac, too—that effrontery. The road went by the lagoon. Keller could see the black sea slugs on the bottom; kindred, these. He wanted to withdraw, like the hermit crab, into a tenement of shade. Balancing his trust in his arms, he remembered, imperfectly, the movie about Frankenstein. Wasn't there a scene where a dead girl was being borne through a town? There was round dancing in the street. It must have been a holiday. The rounds broke up as the solemn man and the girl passed through them. Who was it that was carrying the child, the father or the monster? At any rate, wasn't the monster a kindly person who had been misjudged? I mean,

Keller thought, he had been treated badly, misunderstood; they had all turned against him, hadn't they?

Keller writes in his notebook: "My daughter has run away from home. Beneath the lemon-yellow-and-white canopy, her covers are smooth and empty. No one has ever slept there. I look in my son's room. He lies sprawled upon his bed as though he had been flung down from a great height. I go into the kitchen and hear the refrigerator's reassuring hum. On the counter is an unfinished jigsaw puzzle we were working on, once upon a time, the three of us. We were looking one evening for the dancing green men with the flat bottoms that made up a corner and Benjamin Franklin's coat."

Keller never married and he does not have any children. He writes, with fraudulence and innocence, in his notebook because he feels those in the launch expect him to do something professional—and to remember what never happened or to forget what has. How often can he take the child's vanishing pulse, feel her head? What is left? External cardiac massage? Mouth-to-mouth breathing? Tracheotomy? A drop of sweat falls and lodges along the gold rim at the bottom of one of the lenses of his sunglasses. It shimmers there, creating a spectrum. Keller is diverted. Refraction makes the rim appear to be a chain of gold coins; a sun-ken treasure, Keller thinks. He knows the child has died, but it is still his secret.

Keller writes in his notebook: "I love you."

He drops the notebook overboard. He hears several splashes and sees that the boats have drifted apart and men are diving into the lagoon like Greeks after the cross. No. I did it on purpose. I don't want it. I don't need it any longer. Please don't bring it back to me. It doesn't make any difference. Why do you all have to be so kind? He has seen these people dive and imagines them kicking powerfully toward the bright bottom, the notebook sinking beyond them into the sea's high, inviolate vault. They will never recover it. If the hydrographic chart is right, it is fifteen fathoms deep where the flying boat lands.

Keller continues to hear splashes and opens his eyes; he had not known they were shut. The men are swimming on the surface. The notebook was too light and gaudy to sink. One of them has it now and is returning to the launch. Had they radioed for the flying boat, after all? They had been waiting for him to drop it over the side, throw it away like a murder weapon, and now they are bringing it back—he has it between his teeth—to comfort and condemn him with.

A Description of a Presumption

I am in receipt of twenty packs of sweet, dark Mexican cigarettes called Faros; three cents for sixteen, I'm told. They are, in that sense, a bargain, but I really have no use for them. The illustration on the package, however, is queer and compelling. It shows, in orange and blue, with a great deal of black hatching, a seacoast. The shipping lanes thereabouts must be hazardous, for not one but three lighthouses are pictured—hence "Faros," Spanish for "Lighthouses." One rises in the right foreground, partially cut off by the rectangle of rope, with several fancy knots, that frames the lurid and melancholy scene. Another lighthouse is situated on a small island in the middle ground, and the third is in the distance, near the horizon and imperfectly descried. Although the time is day—the sky is a screen of blue dots, while the sea is solid blue, and consequently darker—the lights of the two nearest lighthouses are shining. The artist has portrayed the effulgent beams by a sequence of orange dashes reminiscent, in a way, of the radiant gaze of Felix the Cat. The far lighthouse and some rocks about it are obscured by a man's hat, and it is not clear whether the artist intended its light to be lit.

Two steamboats are passing in the channels between the lighthouses, and there is an equivocal wind. Dark columns of smoke from the funnels of the inshore ship are billowing abaft, while the pennants on the mast tops and a flag at the bow are blowing in the opposite direction. The shore is barren and rocky, perhaps volcanic, and the sea is rough; there are whitecaps beyond the middle lighthouse, and next to the shore the turbulence is indicated by black smudges that represent waves or their shadows. The illustration may depict an actual view on the Mexican coast, or elsewhere, but here I have no knowledge.

The man in the hat stands in the left foreground, cut off at the back by the rope frame and at the waist by the words "*Cía. Cigarrera.*" In this respect, he is like a ruined bust recovered by divers from the sea, but he was never a hero or a statesman. He is in profile, and his face, which is colored a vivid orange, as though he were looking into a furnace, is similar to one on a playing card: a sulky mouth and several stiff, romantic lashes radiating from a single, inflexible eye. He is facing the first lighthouse but is staring beyond it, fashionably dressed in a jacket, a vest, a necktie, a white shirt, and a jaunty fedora with a turned-down brim. A small cigar or cigarette protrudes, at right angles to his jaw, from the center of his mouth, and he is touching, with his left hand, the brim of his hat. Is he about to tip it to someone or is he merely holding it down against the wind? I would say he is in his early thirties—my age and years of indulgent sorrow.

Is he the keeper of the first lighthouse? He is too elegant, and there is a softness to his round cheek. Is he, rather, a minor official who has the maintenance of all three lighthouses in his trust? The artist has made no connection between the man and his work—the way, for example, in English paintings of the eighteenth century, a keeper or stableboy handles or regards his dogs or horses. The man is a visitor to the coast.

An idle and impatient resident of a large city near the lighthouses, he has often come out on Sundays to this headland to consider the sea and the shipping. The forces of tide and strong winds, the departure of ships, the gift and pledge of the horizon have acted upon him. Today he left forever his apartment—high ceilings, high blue mirrors—that overlooked a square and an ornate fountain where water gushes prodigally from the astonished mouths of stone dolphins with the sound of adoration. His trunks are labelled and a taxi is waiting; he will sail upon the last tide. He knows he has wasted his life: flattered and shielded by women, his easy talents shedding light, like the lighthouses, on that which was already illuminated. Calling upon the coast for the last time, he faces the city and tips his hat in an intransigent salute of farewell.

But this morning he stood at the foot of my bed in the place of drowned men, hat in his hands. I saw him for a moment in the unendurable revelation of full face. He was older than I expected—worn down, too, and full of regret.

"What right do you have," he said bitterly, "to put yourself in my place?"

Chico King, Popular Singer

Chico King keeps a scale in his bedroom in Hollywood Hills. You have, no doubt, seen ones like it on subway platforms or in front of candy stores: "Your Wate and Fate" is painted on one side, " 'Weigh' Your Fate" on the other. For a penny, you get your correct weight and, when a little door flies open, the answer to a trivial question of fact, e.g., "What Aquatic Bird Does Not Fly?"; or advice on a personal problem, e.g., "Why Does Kindness Affect Me?"; or the meaning of a dream, e.g., "I Dreamed I Was Mad." Each of these penny oracles has more than two hundred responses or revelations. Some of them are facetious. For instance, the reply to "Where Do I Find Happiness?" is "Under H, in the Dictionary." On occasion, however, they are threatening. If you choose "I Dreamed of Night," as Chico sometimes does, you will learn that "Misfortune Is Your Lot."

Chico got the scale to amuse chicks, but nowadays he often weighs himself when he is alone and cannot sleep, when he is agitated by obscure or uncertain regrets and longings. He stands naked (except for a pair of half glasses, with heavy, dark rims, and a gold Star of David, which he wears on a fine chain about his neck) and musing on the machine, holding a tall vodka and Bitter Lemon in one hand, and, without hope, drops penny after penny into the slot with the other. He feels, at times, like a jockey weighing out after an unsuccessful and uneventful race. His weight is usually a hundred thirty-four pounds (which, a table on the scale informs him, is below average for his height—five feet seven—and age—forty-one) and, by now, he knows by heart that it is the cooler areas on the sun's surface that make sunspots, that he will meet his master in the opposite sex, and, far from impressing people, his boasting only causes distress.

Several times during the past months, Chico King has seen himself in the distance: once at La Scala; another time in the clubhouse at Santa Anita; and, again, in a parking lot at Dodger Stadium. The person he thinks is himself is always walking casually toward him. As soon as he gets a good look at him, Chico realizes he has been mistaken, that it is a total stranger. Although it is an eerie experience, he is never unsettled by it. In the instant that Chico is convinced that he will be greeting himself, it is, as he has told a couple of shrinks with whom he discussed it at cocktail parties, a gas. As Chico says, it is only the frequency of these incidents, and the fact that they may be of some interest to medical science, that makes him corner and pump the shrinks. "I sincerely hope I am not bugging you, Doctor," says Chico King.

One of the psychiatrists—he was wearing a class ring and Chico wondered whether it was a sign of immaturity—told him: "I'm just speaking off the cuff, but this whole thing sounds very narcissistic. It could be some kind of wish fulfillment. What a relief it must be to meet someone else just like yourself. Very relaxing and pleasant. How nice it must be to meet me. How nice I look. Not so? Maybe younger or better-looking? I think you're exceedingly critical of people, friend. . . ."

"*Comme ci, comme ça*, and the name's Chico, Doctor."

"You put them down, on the one hand, but on the other, the opposite extreme, you're not nearly as good as you want yourself to be. This illusion has the earmarks of a wishing ideal. It suggests you have no realistic picture of yourself. You underevaluate yourself or you overevaluate yourself. Have I struck a chord?"

The other psychiatrist, whom Chico had drawn outside by the pool for, as Chico put it, "frankly, a kind of intimate chat," said: "It is a depersonalization, Mr. King. A transient disturbance which occurs when a person feels estranged from his body, or part of it. Of course, this is a flagrant example, perhaps a stage of regression. Phenomena like this take place more often in dreams. It could be what we call a night residue, as in dreams we have day residues. Do you follow me? It is a disturbance of consciousness; for an instant, the mind functions on a more depressed level. It is a fuguelike state. Perhaps it is a transient uncertainty about who you are. Interestingly, we all have a universal wish to have a twin. It would make life so much simpler to have a ready-made pal, wouldn't it?"

"Do you think it's serious, Doctor?"

"Don't worry."

Chico King, which is not the name he was born with, lies on a massage table in the Kismet Hotel Health Club (With Sauna) in Las Vegas, contemplating, with immeasurable dejection, a map of Finland. Although the health club is in the basement and at the back of the hotel, Chico can hear the mechanical Arab who rides the mechanical camel that plods everlastingly in place by the entranceway. "Howdy, effendi," the Arab booms over and over, like some kind of muezzin, from his seat on the vibrating hump. "Come on in."

Chico King has a terrible hangover and—maybe—a sprained ankle. Last night Chico's pop had him over to the layout Chico bought him in Bel Air. Bewildered and saddened by the unvarying climate, silence, and splendor, the old man spends his days sitting by the pool in a Sy Devore cabaña set, morosely and audibly experimenting with his new full denture, playing gin for a fifth of a cent a point with the gardener or the pool service man, and keeping up a scrapbook on his son, the popular singer, that he started with a two-column ad from a Friday *Mirror*—an imperfectly silhouetted head shot of Chico; great piles of dark, romantic hair; "Sal & Vinnie's Royal Crest Lounge on King's H'way. Wang Is Back with His Exotic Cantonese Cuisine. Groups Invited."

"Pop," Chico once told his father, "you don't have to do the scrapbook. There's a girl at the agency does it, she's paid." "I'm a snipper," his father said. "Clipper," Chico said. "They call it clipping, Pop. Clips." "I'm a ripper," the old man said defiantly, tearing a page out of the *Herald-Examiner* as though he were abrogating a treaty. ("Pop's a gas," Chico tells his hair stylist.) That's a fancy conversation for Chico's pop. He hasn't had much to say since his wife died five years ago and Chico "deported" him, as he has told the pool service man more than once, with more grief than irony, from

Neptune Avenue, Coney Island. Not that, in truth, Chico's pop was ever a conversationalist. At one time in his life he had *schlepped* across the beach at Coney in cutoff pants, selling Fudgsicles from two shopping bags laden with dry ice. "Hey! Fudgie-wudgie!" was all he would cry all weekend, like another kind of muezzin. About all Chico's pop says nowadays is: "How you doing? How's everything? Doing O.K.? All right." He runs them together dispiritedly, without expectation of an answer.

That was what he asked Chico the night before while the carillon set off by the doorbell played the sentimental theme from Chico's first Gold Record. After dinner, the old man challenged his son to "a lee-tle game of croquet." "I'm not half bad at lee-tle games, Pop," Chico said. "For money," Chico's pop said. "You're on for a nickel a stroke," said Chico King.

They played in the dark on the fragrant and mysterious lawn that seemed to have been sodded from a back yard of the past; in Flushing, some dim, leafy place like that; a birdbath full of old leaves and the pink and yellow scraps of pari-mutuel tickets. Chico was carrying, besides his mallet, a tall vodka and Bitter Lemon. Beyond the hedges, he could hear sprinklers and air-conditioners; they sounded to him like deep, significant engines that turned the earth. His father was soon whacking the ball what seemed miles ahead or, at times, when the lawn unexpectedly tilted, miles beneath him ("Pop's a madman at croquet," Chico tells his houseman, whom he calls Cato, although that is not his name.) Chico's pop wore lilac Daks that glowed elusively, beckoningly, in the distance. He had to catch up. Chico caught his foot in the third wicket and silently fell, twisting an ankle. He lay on his side in the comfortable grass and gratefully closed his eyes. Chico's pop wasn't aware that his son had fallen. He had been left behind. Chico could hear his father striking his ball far off.

"What's that, New Hampshire or something?" Chico King asks Carl, the masseur.

"Ha. Ha. Ha, Mr. King," says Carl, who has persuaded himself that he has a lot of personality "That's Finland, the Land of a Thousand Lakes. There's more," he adds, winking. Carl is a successful winker; he practiced in front of a mirror when he discovered he was a slow runner and had failed, after many attempts, to whistle through his teeth.

"You from Finland, Carl?"

"Ha. Ha. Ha, Mr. King," Carl says. "You're a pearl. I'm from Utica Avenue, myself."

"*Landsmann*," Chico says, his depression deepening, as though he has recalled a logical but otherwise unredeeming dream.

"Is that right!" Carl says with, Chico feels, too much astonishment. It is, almost, American history! They may even be teaching it in school systems, for Christ's sake! He knows, for a fact, that his birthplace was once a multiple-choice question in a *Time* current-affairs quiz. Indianapolis; Rome, Georgia; and Havana had been the incorrect responses.

Carl tells him to turn over, and Chico submits pessimistically. He wonders which way he is lying. In Hollywood Hills he lies with his head to the north, and it consoles and orients him to believe that on a strange bed, in a different city, he is still pointing north. Carl is saying that the boss, who is in San Francisco for a Giants game and to pick up the olive branches with which he and Carl flail the customers in the sauna, isn't from Finland, either; the health club had been decorated by a former concessionaire who became oppressed by the desert and took it out by whipping the clientele too harshly. There had been some complaints.

The lights go out as Carl is kneading Chico's right leg.

"I've gone blind," Chico cries.

"Ha. Ha. Ha," says Carl in the dark.

"I've been meaning to ask you . . ." Chico says. The health club is spooky and confidential now, a place for secrets, schemes, and the disclosure of sorrows.

"Yes, Mr. King?"

"What the hell's with the 'ha-ha's'?"

"That's my cheerful, cultivated personality," Carl says. "It's the bit for clientele relations, am I right? I took a twenty-six-week correspondence course by mail from L.A. on redirecting my personality. I can show you some of the literature, if you desire, Mr. King."

"How about the lights, for now?"

"Power," Carl says, convincingly. "I'll lay you this whole side of The Strip is dark past the 'Trop.' But you and I, Mr. King, we can do our work in the dark just as good, isn't it the truth?"

"Yes, Carl," Chico says. He remembers, years ago, a prom date at a small college in upstate New York; a toilet, it was, at best. The boys in the band wore lavender jackets with no collars that year. The lights had gone out in the middle of "Night and Day" and he could hear the kids rushing toward the bandstand in the dark. Like a canary in a mine, he could smell the couples crowded in front of him, swaying, he knew, arms about one another. The mike was dead, but he had finished the set; he felt bold and sublime, like a religious leader or a liberator.

Carl's hands—heavy, public, and disembodied—pause on Chico's legs as though Carl, too, is hearing standards from far off; ballrooms where colored lights revolve, and roller-skating rinks booming like the resonant chambers of the sea. Upstate New York is more mysterious and remote than Finland, Chico thinks; so many little towns no one ever heard of up there; where Dick Diver went from place to place; not a winner, poor kid. Chico has been reading good books lately and is taking dramatic coaching. He has told his agent that he is through with the Mickey Mouse parts and is available for roles with some red meat on the bone. It was in the columns that Chico King wants to do Prince Myshkin.

"Would you favor me with a rendition of one of your numbers, Mr. King?" Carl asks. "I've got all your records at home from the beginning."

Chico never does benefits unless it is a big Jewish or interracial *tsimmes* at Madison Square Garden or the Hollywood Bowl, or a telethon for an incurable disease that bumps off one out of every hundred kids, sooner or later; those are really terrible things; kids hopping around on shiny little crutches; could be Scott or Kelly, God forbid. Sometimes, however, late at night, when he is drunk or afflicted with passion or the fear of slipping, he sings for a head he is trying to make, although these urgent, despondent ballads have led to three lousy marriages and dozens of otherwise nice kids who couldn't put the cap back on the toothpaste, and were inspired to do clumsy pirouettes in his Charvet dressing gown in front of his triple mirror.

Some years ago, Chico had told a reporter from *Life* —a very sensitive, perceptive kid, but bad legs—the whole unfortunate *megillah* of his preadolescence: eating two-day-old bread and tomato herring for dinner; hiding behind the sprung sofa chair playing his only record on his toy Victrola—"I hear Miss Liberty, She is calling me—"; and having an inferiority complex.

The bit about Miss Liberty was lifted from someone else's childhood (a comic he worked with in the mountains used it in a routine), but he wanted the kid to have a good write-up.

Chico remembers that the reporter had asked him: "What was it that motivated you, Mr. King? What was the impulse or foundation for, or of, your ambition and drive?"

The interview had occurred in Miami Beach, where he was making a personal appearance—as a favor. He was lying on an adjustable chaise on the sun deck of a hotel on Collins Avenue, holding a reflector about his face. Cha-cha lessons were being given at the pool's edge.

"It wasn't money, which I know you're thinking," he had told her. "To be perfectly sincere and frank with you, honey, it was power, the power that is the handmaiden of fame."

"Power?" she said.

"Power," he said.

"What did you want to accomplish with this power, Mr. King?"

"To get chicks," Chico said. "When I was a kid, I couldn't get no chicks. I don't know why I'm telling you this. It's in the strictest confidence, so don't quote me, honey."

"What can I write?" she asked.

"I hope you sympathize with the position I'm in,"

he said. "You understand that I inadvertently bared my heart. I'm a very feeling guy. Write this, sweetheart. I wanted to prove something to myself, something terribly tangible. Scratch it. Say I wanted to give my parents the worldly goods to which they were unaccustomed, blah, blah, blah."

"I'm disappointed in you, Chico," she said.

"How's that?" he said, rolling over on his stomach.

"I'm sorry," she said. "I said—"

"Forget it, honey. I'm disappointed in myself, too. How's about a little drinkie, cha-cha-cha?"

For some reason, Chico lets Carl have a verse and a chorus of "Night and Day." He knows he wouldn't have done it if the lights hadn't been out, if the health club hadn't been so reverberant; he likes his sound down here. When he is finished, he feels he has given something of himself away and is irreparably diminished. Carl has taken advantage of him, laid out as he is here, naked and tragic in the dark like a Greek on a shield before a burning city on a plain. That role would be a gas if he had a build.

"Encore! Encore!"

Someone he hasn't noticed is reclining in the corner. Chico raises himself on his elbows and tries to make him out. All he can see are the monstrous and incomprehensible folds of a sheet. The interloper looks like an iceberg must at night—dreadful and unfounded.

"Hey, friend, encore! Encore!"

He sounds like the first shrink, the one with the ring and the narcissism scene. It's not impossible he should be in Vegas. He wore a silk suit to that party—one hell of an outfit for any kind of sincere psychiatrist.

"I will always cherish and revere this moment, Mr. King," says Carl.

An hour after he has left the Kismet Hotel Health Club, Chico King is wandering discontentedly in the desert, carrying a 9-iron like a crook or staff, and looking for a lost ball. Here, in this pale, difficult, and Biblical wilderness out of bounds, he feels reverent and anchoritic, as though the object of his devious search is not a Titleist 3, but The Word. He sees himself, in the complimentary light of early evening, wearing a brilliant robe and a *Hasidisher* beard, accompanying Chuck Heston to The Last Supper.

The pro of the par-3 Greensleeves Hotel and Country Club course had offered to go around with Chico, but Chico chose to play alone; he was still pondering the apparition of the shrink in the basement, and other untimely visitations. Chico lost his first Titleist off the first tee when, choking down on his wedge in an effort to punch the ball to the green, he had, instead, skulled it into the swimming pool of one of the Tudor-type villas that adjoined the course. Chico called it a mulligan and played another ball. On the third hole he hooked a

9-iron into the desert. He had been determined to find and play his ball, ignoring the two-stroke penalty for hitting out of bounds, but spiritually uplifted by his vision on the sand, he limps back to the third tee. This time he slices the ball into a corner of an empty water hazard. The concrete bottom of the pond is coated with mud and an inch or two of putrid water in which Chico's ball lies partially submerged, a few feet from shore. Chico sees there are two ways to make this shot to the green to his right: he can either wade out into the slime, or he can stand on the dry base of the sloping concrete wall and hit the ball left-handed. He chooses the latter, but since he doesn't want to chance a shot with the club face reversed, he decides to try blasting out of the muck with his putter. He swings vengefully, the ball explodes from the pond, flies over the bank, and lands, out of sight, on the green. Chico is drenched, but he is elated. It is, undeniably, the finest recovery he has ever made. He wishes the pro had tagged along so he could have seen just how pretty it was.

As Chico is lining up his putt, the automatic sprinkler system that waters the course comes on. All around the elevated green, hidden nozzles rise out of the fairways, lashing them with powerful jets of water. Chico looks for a way back to the clubhouse, but as soon as he discovers a dry path, more sprinklers emerge like a sudden and confounding infestation of snakes, and his escape routes are cut off. He is surrounded, unprepared and hopeless, without a raven or a dove trembling on his fingers. The golf course is underwater.

"Mr. Chico King, telephone. Mr. Chico King, telephone, please."

He is being paged over the public-address system. As he plunges desperately through the flood to the clubhouse, the great, anonymous voice sounds to his ears like the Call to Judgment.

"We didn't see you out there, Mr. King," the pro says. "Get lost?"

"I was in the interior of one of your filthy lakes," says Chico—his George Sanders imitation.

"We couldn't have turned it off, anyway," the pro says. "It's automatically set to go, progressively, at 18:45 hours, sharpereenie. It's all programmed. A course like this drinks up one heck of a lot of aqua pura, Mr. King."

"Don't mention it, kid," Chico says, picking up the phone and asking for his page. It is Arlene, the first of his three wives. She lives in Paradise Valley with Scott and Kelly and her new husband, a 21-dealer at the Kismet. Arlene is calling to tell Chico she has heard he is in town and that today is his daughter Kelly's ninth birthday.

Richard, Arlene's husband, is sitting on the front step of his house as Chico limps across the lawn, carrying Suzy Sez, a talking doll. Richard is wearing a gold-

and-purple softball uniform. "Kismet" is written across the chest in a mock-Arabic typeface called Legend. Richard has a new fielder's mitt and is punching it to make a pocket. When he sees Chico approaching, he picks up a softball and, yelling, "Hey, Chico, baby boy, little pepper, baby," fires it at him. Chico neither expects nor sees the ball, and it strikes him in the temple and he falls once more, Suzy Sez in his arms.

When he comes to, he sits up on the lawn and sees Richard and Arlene looking down at him.

Richard: Jesus, I'm sorry.

Chico: When you going to grow up, Richard?

Arlene: Don't you recognize your father, Kelly?

Kelly (who has run up with Scott): Maybe.

Chico: My little sweetheart! (He holds out his arms —a blind and legless beggar; his shades, which had been knocked off by the softball, lie on the lawn beyond his reach. Kelly shrinks back and hugs Arlene.) How come Kelly's wearing glasses, Arlene?

Kelly: I have a slight astigmatism.

Scott: Why are you sitting in the middle of the lawn, Father? There's dew.

Chico: I'm waiting for my little apple dumpling to give her poor, old, suffering dada a kiss.

Arlene: Kiss your father, darling. He only bites when he hasn't been fed.

Kelly: He looks different on "The Ed Sullivan Show."

Arlene: Only taller.

Richard: Jesus, Chic', I thought you heard me.

(Kelly kisses Chico.)

Scott: What's with the doll, Father?

Chico: It's for my little sunshine on her birthday.

Kelly: Can I play with her now?

Chico: Her name is Suzy Sez.

Kelly: I like her hair. (She strokes it.)

Arlene: It's the children's dinnertime, Chico. You can play with it later, Kelly.

Richard: Can I help you up, old man? (He takes hold of Chico under the arms.)

Chico: Touchies off!

Richard: Je-sus! I was only trying to help.

Chico: Help I don't need. If you don't mind, Kelly and I are going to sit out here on this pretty lawnie and play make-believe housie with this bee-you-ti-ful talking doll.

Kelly: What does she say, Daddy?

Arlene: Chico, I would rather you played *later on*. It's *time* for their *din*ner. Anyhoo, you look like a ludicrous jerk sitting there in the dark.

Richard: She's right, Chico.

Scott: What's ludicrous?

Chico: Listen to me, Arlene. This is my sensational daughter and I'm her goddam father, and if I want to sit out here on your lawn and listen to what this doll has to say . . . (Kelly begins to cry. Arlene takes her by the arm and escorts her toward the house. Richard and Scott follow.)

Arlene (over her shoulder): When you decide to stand up and become a civilized human being, you can join us for din-din.

Chico: Kelly! (The front door closes. He is abandoned and bereft. He takes one of the doll's records out of his pocket and, lifting Suzy's smock, jams it in. He pulls the cord in her back.)

Suzy: People just worship the ground you stand on. The President invited me to the White House. My picture was on the cover of *Life*. Everybody loves me. Say "cheese"; we're posing for pictures. Don't you think I'm beautiful? I think you're so talented.

(Chico gets up and goes into the house, leaving the doll on the lawn. Richard, Kelly, Scott, and Arlene are sitting in the dining alcove eating spaghetti.)

Chico: Arlene, I'm terribly sorry. Richard, I'm terribly sorry. Kelly and Scott, I'm terribly sorry, likewise. I've had, with one truly unforgettable exception, a really terrible day, today.

Richard: How's about a little drink, Chico? (He rises in anticipation.)

Chico: A little drinkie would be grand, old man. How's the old ball?

Richard: We're in first, Chico.

Chico: That's really sensational, Richard. And how's the old average?

Richard: Well, I'm not playing regularly. (He hands Chico his drink.)

Chico: I'm truly sorry to hear that you're riding the

bench this season, Richard. I was thinking, Arlene, that it being my daughter's birthday, I'd like to take the kids out for a Coke or something—after dinner.

Scott: I want a tall Roy Rogers with crunched ice.

Kelly: They make divoon Shirley Temples at Donald's Supper Club.

Chico: Supper club!

Arlene: On Tropicana. It's just a roadhouse.

Richard: I've got to go to work, if you'll excuse me, so count me out.

Arlene: We'd love to go. Do you want some spaghetti?

Chico: No, thank you, but it really smells sensational, Arlene.

Kelly: Do we have time to go outside and play horsie, Daddy?

Chico: All the time in the blue-eyed world, pumpkin pie.

Kelly: I've got a whip and everything. Come on, Scott.

Scott: I'm not getting down on my hands and knees.

Kelly: No, you're going to be a *show* horse. First, you start off running wild, and then I find you and catch you and whip you and stuff. (They run outside. Richard goes into the master bedroom. From time to time he is heard singing "On the Road To Mandalay.")

Chico: And how's the blue-eyed world been treating you, Arlene?

Arlene: Just swimmingly, thank you. So what are you doing in town?"

Chico: Pop and I were playing a little low-stake croquet last night and I thought I'd fly over after the game.

Arlene: How's Pop?

Chico: Making it. So anyway, what's with Kelly's eyes, Arlene? I never heard no nothing about eyes. I got this specialist in Westwood, and if you'd only have kept me informed once in a while, I'd have had her flown in for a thorough examination.

(The children return.)

Kelly: The horsie game wasn't a success. Scott kept trying to choke me.

Chico: That's life, kids.

Richard (entering): Goom-bye, everybody. (He is wearing a white-on-white shirt with a long, slightly soiled collar, and a black necktie decorated with an Arab on a camel, a pair of dice showing craps, a fan composed of an ace of spades and a king of spades, a leaning tower of chips, and a roulette wheel.) Don't do anything I wouldn't do.

Chico: My, you're looking lovely tonight, Richard. I may drop by the Kismet later.

Richard: I wish you wouldn't play with me, Chico. You know, they frown on that.

Chico: And that's life for you, Richard. (He rises and fixes himself another drink.) So anyway, after I finish this little refill, what say we make the scene at Donald's?

Scott: Would you like to see my scorpion, Father?

Chico: There is nothing that I would rather look at in the whole world. (Scott hands him a jar filled with formaldehyde. Within it, a large scorpion is rapturously curled, its stinger imbedded in its abdomen. Whatever actually took place, it seems that on account of some inexplicable torment or ecstasy, the scorpion turned upon itself and filled its simple system with its own venom.)

Scott: I found it in the desert.

Chico: It's dead.

Scott: What did you think?

Chico: I think that's life, too.

As Arlene is saying for the fourth time at Donald's Supper Club, that isn't everything going just swimmingly—if that be the case, Chico thinks, becoming drunk, then I am side-stroking in the middle of the Arctic Ocean—the lights go out, Chico moans, a record of "Happy Birthday To You," as sung by Chico King in the winter of 1952, and one of his very worst sellers, plays and a procession, led by Donald and Mrs. Donald, and composed, in the following order, of the hostess, six waitresses, the bartender, the chef, the second cook, the salad man, the dishwasher, and two porters, emerges from the kitchen singing along with the record. Donald is bearing a birthday cake.

"Who else has a birthday today?" says Kelly.

"Only you, darling," says Arlene.

Donald places the cake in front of Kelly.

"You rotten bitch," says Chico, in his Ronald Colman accent. "You stabbed me behind my back. They got the recording off of you!"

He tries to get up, but the parade is marching raggedly around the table and he is hemmed in.

"It is, indeed, a great privilege for us to have you with us tonight in our little supper club, Mr. King," says Donald. "Would you do us the honor of helping your birthday girl cut the first slice?"

"Up yours, Donald," Chico says. "The party's over, so will you break it up so I can go to the can."

Chico sits in the locked commode, investigating the tiled floor. He once had discovered camels and seacoasts among tiles, lost children and the ravaged profiles of world leaders (of course, as he had told the kid from *Life*, the little boy's room was at the end of the hall in those days, and everybody brought his own paper), but here the floor is unrevealing. The men's room smells of floral air freshener, there are great floes in the urinals, and no one has written anything on the walls.

Chico wonders what innocent and unencumbered travellers have sat here before him, bent in agony, a lethal ray at his back purifying the seat (it is forbidden to look at its mysterious source), at his sides the inexpressive walls, before him the impassable door. If he had a ballpoint and a gift he would fill the spaces with divoon indulgences, and a sermon on something or other. He has been struck down and blinded, but what has he to confess? Is it wrong to try to overtake your father in the night, to presume *not* to walk on water? He has worshipped false idols and been misled by benign strangers.

From this white, glaring cell he could be starting forth anew, a kind of vital Schweitzer and archbishop of the north, conveyed through the snow on a sleigh pulled by two white camels, their mingled vapors and the bells on the harness signalling his coming. He would visit his remote and scattered communicants and, elevated and infallible on the sleigh, dispense Milky Ways to the pious children, antibiotics to the sick, blessings to the good, penances to the bad, while a heavenly choir sang a deeply felt number by a Tiomkin. His robes and rugs, his sparkling mitre, would make him appear tall, broad, and inflexible, richly dark and inaccessible, too, in this pacific archdiocese of snow and ice. What kind of shades does an archbishop wear, anyway?

"Are you all right?"

"Who's there?"

"Me."

"Who is me?"

"Scott, Father. Ma says if you're through, she'd like you to drive us home. She says not to let you slide the car keys under the door. Are you all right?"

"Are you getting good marks?"

"Sure, Father, but why?"

"Because you are fabulously perceptive, my son."

"It's too late to play games, Father. Come out."

"Come out, come out, wherever you are."

"Come on."

"Here I come, ready or not," says Chico, and fearfully opens the door.

After he has driven them all home, Chico sits in his car watching their lights go on and off. It must be like that at the bottom of the sea, with all those stupendous and insatiable fish lit up like marquees colliding down there. He hears a child's voice.

"Are you afraid of the bogeyman?" it asks with sweet precision. "Don't be a fraidy cat. Don't be a fraidy cat . . ." It is Suzy Sez, Chico decides, retrieved from the lawn. He had never shown Kelly how to make her work, and now the record is stuck.

"Money plays," says Chico King, putting a hundred-dollar bill on the table.

"Money plays," says Richard.

He sweeps up the cards that have been spread out before him as if in the first stage of some unaccountable trick, shuffles them, and places the deck in front of Chico. Chico raps it with a knuckle.

"Please cut, Mr. King," says Richard.

"How you been keeping, Mr. King?" says the pit boss.

"*Comme ci, comme ça*, Bruno," says Chico. "Could you send Bonnie over?"

Bruno depresses his snapper and a cocktail waitress costumed like an odalisque approaches the 21 table.

"Good evening, Mr. King," says Bonnie. "What would you like tonight?"

"I'd like to have a party with you, Bonnie," says Chico.

" 'Arf, arf,' says Sandy, Mr. King."

"So it shouldn't be a total loss, I'll have a tall vodka and Bitter Lemon."

"Will you please cut the deck, Mr. King," says Richard.

"Why not, Richard. So anyway, how's every little thing, Bruno?"

"Swimming, Mr. King. You lately?"

"Swimming, likewise, Bruno."

Richard deals. Chico signals for Richard to come again by scraping his cards on the table.

"Have you ever considered, Bruno, that this gesture here is like a dog covering up his do?"

"You're a pearl, Mr. King," says Bruno.

"You really think so, Bruno?"

Chico busts out.

"Tall vodka and Bitter Lemon, Mr. King," says Bonnie.

"Thank you, cupcake," says Chico, tipping her. "Money plays."

"Money plays," says Richard.

"Why don't you think Bonnie'll have a party with me, Bruno?"

"You got me there now, Mr. King. I couldn't imagine for the world."

"That's life, isn't it, Bruno? You never know, do you?"

Chico busts out again.

"Bruno, what aquatic bird does not fly?"

"I don't get you, Mr. King."

"Let me ask you this, you dumb son of a bitch: what will you make my chances of redemption—2-12? Or, how many points will you give me—I got beatification and you got self-immolation?"

"You all right, Mr. King?"

"It's very sweet of you to inquire, Bruno. Did you know that if you dreamed you were mad it was a good sign for all? Seriously now, what do you think of me?"

"I always catch your act whenever I can, you know that, Mr. King."

"I thought you was an entertainer, friend."

Another player has sat down at the 21 table.

"You know, Doctor," says Chico, "I'm deeply indebted to you. Bruno, I want to introduce you to a prominent shrink from the L.A. area, Dr. I've-never-had-the-pleasure-I'm-sure."

"Glad to meet you, I'm sure, Doctor," says Bruno.

On the revolving lounge stage, fifteen harmonica

players with sequined tails are playing Ravel's "Bolero."

"Doctor, don't you think it would be a miracle cure for my terminal case of narcissism if I had a party with Bonnie?"

"I know I seen you some place, friend."

"Bruno, do you think Richard cheats the players or the house? If you can answer in three-tenths of a second it's an indoor record."

"Did I ever see you on *Stump the Stars*?"

"I think Richard's a son-of-a-bitching cheat," says Chico. "You said I was extremely critical of people, Doctor. That's why I owe you something. For a starter how would you like a punch on your prominent Jewish nose, you fruit?"

"Hey, what are you nuts or what?"

"Don't you think you ought to go to bed, Mr. King?" Bruno says. "You've been doing pretty good with the glass."

"I never sleep, Bruno. That's the secret of my success. Do you think I'd be beloved by millions if I even slept a wink? I'm going to rap you in the *kishkes*, Doctor, because you're a molester of helpless little adults, and because you got a secret Captain Midnight mirror on your ring, and you're reading the cards. That makes you a son-of-a-bitching cheat, did you know that?"

"Please, Mr. King, don't middle me," says Bruno. "Go to bed, for sweet Christ's sake."

"Jesus!" says the second player.

"Worship in the church of your choice on Sunday, my son," says Chico rising, and drops a twenty-five-dollar chip in Richard's breast pocket, as though it were a poor box.

The valet brings Chico his car and Chico flips him a silver dollar. As he is about to get into the car, Chico turns toward the multitude that is packed about the entrance waiting for their cars or taxis; the second show has just broken. He empties his pockets and, making the sign of the cross, throws coins and chips at the mob's feet. "Blah, blah, blah, so anyway," he says reverently. As he drives off, he sees himself simply dressed in a valet's white coveralls, standing in the driveway, waving him to the left. Since he hadn't known where he was going, he is grateful for the direction. He carefully makes the turn, steps on the gas, and crashes headlong into the mechanical camel and Arab. The contraption topples and falls apart, revealing an unusually tiny motor. The four red bulbs that were its eyes shine still with a steadfast and devotional light, and its recorded voice repeats over and over: "Effendi. Effendi. Effendi."

Chico King sits in Bruno's office waiting for the girl to put his call through.

"Hey, Pop," Chico says into the phone, "It's me, Chico."

"How you doing? How's everything? Doing O.K.? All right."

"Hey, Pop, I was thinking, how about a lee-tle game of croquet?"

"For money."

"You're on, but leave us not be greedy. Nickel a stroke."

"How soon you be here?"

"Don't worry, Pop."

Silence.

"You there, Pop?"

"Where else would I be?"

"See you, then."

"Not if I see you first, sonny."

"You going L.A. play croquet with your old man?" says Bruno.

"It's better than a jab in the eye with a sharp stick," says Chico.

A Blessed Day

This is my predicament: there is a Cheerio on the bath mat and no one will pick it up.

We live next to the water on pilings, four in a drafty room: me, Margaret, and the contrary kids. At high tide the sea resounds beneath the floor, and all of us have remarked, at one time or another during our vacation, that it is like living on a boat. I said it first, and I am the only one who has made long, illusory passages, heard at nightfall the great exhalation of whales, their profound sighing, and knows what he is talking about. The others have mimicked me, as is so often the case, and here I am trying to recall the last sunny day.

It is Labor Day, and hereabouts summer is over. Any day now, Chooch, the gentle waiter, will drive us home to the city in his Volkswagen; behold us huddled humbly in the back as though in the dark, trucial steerage of the Ark of the Covenant.

Chooch comes every morning in his go-aheads and leaves pie fillings in our refrigerator. One day he brings mocha brandy, another lime chiffon, and sometimes apricot sherry. "I could tell you stories that would make your hair stand on end," he says confidentially.

Yesterday, Chooch and his roommate drove us out to inspect a piece of land they have just bought. The property slopes down from the road and has a cover of bayberry, blueberry, lichen, and a few pines. While Chooch showed us where they are going to build—when they get their hands on the money, as he says, evoking images, somehow, of broken glass and plundering—his roommate sowed bluebell seeds in the valley and planted two peach pits he had saved. Mike, who will soon be my stepson, discovered "rabbit poo," and Patsy, who will soon be my stepdaughter, claimed she was bitten by a red ant.

The reason I mention this outing is that it changed my notion of the future; not, of course, to one that is any more earth-shaking or original than its predecessors. Poking about that undeveloped slope, hearing Chooch describing imaginary evenings when he and his roommate will watch the real view from the sun deck of an imaginary house, made me realize that their future had become, by this purchase, foretold, a commitment and a resignation, as, shortly, will mine. The spaces are now bounded and numbered, and though afflicted by common enough tragedies—the enmity of brothers, a job lost through petulance, giving birth to a monster—you still must fill them in with the proper colors. (I went into an art store the other day, brimming with good will, for I wasn't going to buy anything. "What do you call those sets where you paint by the numbers?" I asked the clerk. "That's it!" he cried. "Painting by the numbers! It's an American tradition.") Was I a sentimentalist to have believed that the future was otherwise, haphazard and opportunistic, full of undiscovered motel rooms, mountain trails where bear poo steams, a vision underwater?

"Chooch," his roommate called up to him, "shall I plant the peach pits together in case one doesn't sprout?"

As Chooch seemed to be deliberating, I replied: "Plant them far apart so they won't die in each other's shade." I saw there was still a choice, in a way.

For the most part, the weather pins us indoors. Mike and Patsy play Apartment Hunting:

Mike: Now here's a nice little apartment, lady.

Patsy: I'm sorry, but it won't be suitable. Not

enough closets. There are *just* not enough closets.

Mike: Watch your mouth, lady.

Margaret (who will soon be my wife) and I have been looking in the city, wandering through vacant apartments stained and littered with the enigmatic clues of departed strangers. Who lived here? Why did they leave? Where have they gone? There is a spot in the foyer. Is it blood or milk? A box of smashed Christmas-tree ornaments is in the bottom of the closet, surf clam shells that were ashtrays lie on the windowsills, a type-writer eraser has sunk in the toilet bowl. We have slowly risen in self-service elevators that reeked faintly of urine and read the arbitrary declarations of love and piety (temptation, too) scratched on the walls; stolen through darkened rooms full of dyed rushes when the tenants were away. Porcelain shepherds and shep-herdesses lust on the dusty mantels; illustrated sex manuals are hidden behind mysteries from The Detec-tive Book Club of Roslyn, L.I.; flannelette pajama bot-toms, their strings missing, hang on bathroom doors; long white hairs are in the sinks; and I smell bacon in the halls. I do not open the blinds and look out the windows. What could be there but areaways and alleys, mosquitoes trying to get in?

How can you keep your wits unless you balance these things? For instance, where I go swimming in the city, a dim, barny place, quiet except for my tedious splash-ing, there is a young man who stands by the side of the pool, his elbows in the gutter. Above his head is a sign that reads: NO LOITERING IN THE SHALLOW WATER. (A praiseworthy precept, and remember, I tell the children, never lend money before you put your socks on.) He talks to himself intently, with gestures. At first, I thought he was some kind of Off Broadway actor rehearsing a part, and I was amused and intrigued. But he has been talking for months, and he surely would have learned his role by now, if he had one. I am apprehensive. I try to hear what he is saying, without success, and watch him out of the corner of my eye as I swim by, wondering what acts of violence he will commit when his words are finally spent or no longer suffice. I go to the barbershop and even the scales. The barbers are all wearing light-blue nylon shirts. "How do you like our new costumes?" my barber asks, pirouetting. I feel like applauding. "Blue cloths, blue towels, everything blue for summer. In the winter, the boss says everything red. *Ma'rone!* Red is for *shoe*makers. Green for winter! Yellow, maybe. How do you like stripes?" The Muzak plays a tango, and in the mirror I behold the barbers dancing behind their customers.

Once in a while Mike composes, with a ballpoint pen, unpopular songs or dirges that will never make the WMCA Good Guys' Survey or become, in time, Golden Oldies. There are four pens, each with a different-colored ink, and they fit into a stand. Margaret bought the set from a deaf-and-dumb man who visited her office and handed her a flier decorated with an American flag and the Pledge of Allegiance on one side and the dactylological alphabet on the other. There was a deaf-and-dumb man who used to visit my dormitory on the mornings before football games, sullenly peddling combs. Perhaps Margaret's is the same one. (It's not too far-fetched, is it? For instance, Margaret tells me she has, over the years, seen Henry, a slow and elderly messenger boy who claims he is Shirley Temple's cousin and is inclined to wish everyone a pleasant afternoon, at the Freeport, L. I., railway station and at the bar of the Great Northern Hotel, where he had been dispatched to fetch an umbrella. On the last occasion, she greeted him. Henry was confused, but only for a moment. "Oh, hello Miss Design Studio, 16 West 45th Street," he said, beaming. "I wish you a pleasant afternoon." Life, I have recently learned, is far from chancy. Its surprises, and there are not many, are more a factor of our faulty or inadequate comprehension of its real nature than any inherent inconstancy. One thing does follow another, but who is willing to take the trouble to make the connection?) I picture the deaf-and-dumb man ascending to Margaret's office, zealous and dejected beneath the human hair that adorns the ceiling of the elevator. What horrors does he imagine in his silence and inarticulation? He does not know yet, as he always works from top to bottom, that they make wigs on the third floor, and hair is everywhere, blown about by fans and drafts. His is no everyday affliction. Would it be presumptuous to assume that he no longer yearns, has abandoned the future as one, without thought, turns off the hot-water faucet, that his ceiling is made of stamped tin, that he has a cardboard wardrobe and cooks soup on a hot plate, comforted by the fragrant steam?

A sample of Mike's songs:

> My father is depressed,
> My mother cooks the meals,
> And I'm a little sandbar
> That plays with the seals.

He sings it to a common melody I cannot place. I have the feeling that to it I marched to war.

From a nearby wharf I can hear the fairies singing, " 'It's a great, wide, wonderful world we live in . . .' " The tide is out and great black-backed gulls are rending a skate far from shore. I am alone, as I once was so often, with little to do, too much to say. Margaret said she was going to look in on Chooch and learn how to make pie fillings; the children said they were off to the Portuguese bakery to buy flipper dough. I have an unreasonable fear that they are not coming back. They had a secret rendezvous at the stand where the jeeps leave for dune rides. Do they have enough money to take the bus to Providence? Margaret has relatives there in a suburb; former in-laws, I believe.

Do you think I'm insincere? Look at what I found this afternoon in "Tales from the Unknown," a comic book. It's a balance sheet the children drew up on me, pro and con, and *who* do you think taught them *those* words?

This is Patsy's:

Pro

1. He has a lot of money.
2. He usually has a close shave.
3. He says excuse me when he burps.

Con

1. He doesn't explain things very well.
2. He says he likes everything when he doesn't.
3. He goes to the bathroom a lot at night.

This is Mike's:

Pro

1. You ask him for something and he gets it for you.
2. He's nice to you.
3. He always knows what time it is.

Con

1. He never smiles.
2. He spends to much.
3. He always gos to the bathroom.

It is obvious that the cons outweigh the pros, and it will all come to a bad end, but how do you like my kids' spelling? Patsy gets an A-plus. Mike made a few mistakes, but Patsy's ten and he's only eight. Give him a B-plus and compliment him on his penmanship. No word from Margaret—who is a good speller, too, has a neat, large, upright hand, and was born under Taurus (her horoscope for today reads: "A short time spent in seclusion will reveal the best path to follow")—but there is no doubt that she is the ringleader and that I will be getting a telegram shortly telling me to pack their bags and ship them to some street or other named after a commonplace tree; plaster ducks and ducklings on the patchy lawns and love letters with deckle edges in the attics. Last night, while we were in the act and obligation of love, she bitterly cried: "Why don't you pay any attention to me?" How could I tell her? I have so much to think about these days and nights: this exacting view of the future, for example; the prevalence of secrets; and other broad, sad currents.

I must have fallen asleep, for the next I knew Margaret was standing by the bed, fully dressed and wearing lipstick. "Where are you going?" I asked. "I'm going for a walk," she said. We are, I sometimes feel, characters who should confide their shame and aspirations to Mary Worth. "But what the hell are you wearing bright-red lipstick for?" I said, afraid and yet, in a way, relieved. Neither of us, circling one another all these months like investigating dogs, at turns wary and reckless, had admitted to ourselves that we might not be inevitably drawing closer with each mutual revolution. It is possible that we are governed by synodic laws and, unaware or ignorant, had missed our most favorable opposition, or, even, that we are eccentric or lawless and growing finally apart. This last eventuality does not, as I have said, entirely unsettle me. If it is true, I am then, at the same time, getting nearer to my former position. Whatever its defects and melancholy airs, it is, at least, familiar. "It's called Crackerjack Red," Margaret told me, and what more could I say? True, I could have leaped out of bed and kissed her, but I don't like the taste of lipstick. Whatever the color, it is reminiscent of wild cherry Life Savers. I decided, considering all things, to go back to sleep.

I seek consolation from mementos and empty my wallet on the table. Here is what I have carried on my hip to this gray and challenging shore:

1. Four tickets reading: "ONE COUPON, BROADWAY PLAYLAND, 1580 BROADWAY. COUPONS REDEEMABLE FOR VALUABLE PREMIUMS. FOR YOUR CONVENIENCE OPEN AN ACCOUNT IN THE PLAYLAND BANK." An excellent suggestion, I believe.

2. The calling card of Lieutenant Colonel L. Frank Burdeen, Royal Canadian Ordnance Corps. He has written "Butterfields Bank, Bermuda," on the back. I met the Colonel on a flight from Papeete to Honolulu. He had a bottle of dark rum in his kit, and we drank it together out of collapsible aluminum cups that he also

provided while he told me about the Vale of Kashmir.

The Colonel said he was about to retire and go live in Bermuda. If I ever found myself there I was to get his address from Butterfields. We wouldn't have much to talk about, though, I suppose. He has already related to me the chief marvels and disappointments of his life, and they are not too different, at that.

3. A piece of ruled notepaper reading: "My IOU to Patsy for $1.00 (One Dollar) is invalid." It is signed "Patsy, 8/24/63" and embellished with flowers and bunny rabbits done in blue and red ink; more evidence of the deaf-and-dumb man. Is it possible, thinking it over, that he lived in one of the gloomy apartments Margaret and I have looked at? Perhaps he became deaf and dumb late in life, lost his job, or gave it up, even, out of shame, paid his rent with savings until they were gone, which brought us to his home and him to the lofts selling ballpoint pens with variously colored inks. I dictated the IOU to Patsy to teach her proper business methods.

4. The stub of a cashier's check for $482.29 drawn by the Union Square Savings Bank. The check was dated 7/30/63 and was payable to my lawyer. Where it says "For," I have written "Margaret's Divorce." How much money have I spent (gone down the drain) on Margaret or given her for rent, Patsy's Stretchini Stretch Nylon Pop-over and Slack Playmates, Mike's apricot rolls? "KEEP THIS RECEIPT," the stub cautions

me. "WE CANNOT GIVE INFORMATION OR SEARCH RECORDS UNLESS IT IS SUBMITTED." I obey. Who can tell? I don't walk when it says "DON'T WALK" or "CARRY ANY LIGHTED CIGAR, CIGARETTE OR PIPE IN OR ON ANY STAIRWAY, PLATFORM, STATION OR CAR OF ANY RAILWAY RUNNING UNDERNEATH THE GROUND SURFACE" or remove the tag from upholstered furniture "UNDER PENALTY OF LAW." I was brought up to never tell a lie and to tie my shoelaces with a double bow.

5. Telephone numbers and addresses:

a. Moira, who—overwhelmed by what?—tried, but failed, to leap from my bedroom window into the trees of heaven.

They are all moving out of my apartment house as though fleeing from the plague. I am convinced something rotten has infested it and measures should be taken. Have you seen them put those great bags over houses and pump poison gas inside to kill the termites? From far off you can hear the compressor going day and night. Cops are always hanging around our lobby talking to one of the 24-Hour Doormen—the one who has so little faith in razor blades he periodically examines them under his microscope, but is the world ready for his findings?—and checking the artificial plants. The superintendent has a furtive look, a foot in a cast, and carries a bayonet in his belt. A murder; two suicides; a natural death in a slumber nook on the eleventh floor, undiscovered for six or seven days; bellowing alcoholics trapped in the laundry room by overflowing foam and remorse; burglaries; poisoned Boston bull terriers; pot parties on the roof; an attempted rape. Peeping Toms creep in their socks up and down the fire stairs or lie in the corridors and peer under doors.

b. Alice, who lived in the 4000's on Camellia Street in North Hollywood, California, her abundant hair in a flowered dryer. She left me one evening to go to the ladies' room of The Stardust Hotel in Las Vegas, and I never saw her again.

c. Sara Ann, who touched the beach with her elbows without bending her knees. I followed her into the surf at Sea Girt, New Jersey, in the summer of the shark scare, and kissed her there before I knew her name; my last inspiration and romantic encounter. The sharks never got her, such were her charms. I received a picture postcard from Sara Ann several months ago. It showed a view of a Hertz office. She wrote that she was teaching tap dancing and ballet in South Miami, and was divorced. I had not known she was married.

d., e., f., et cetera. Like a., b., and c., lost or abandoned, moved away. Strange, impatient men answer their phones, or bewildered children saying, "Daddy, come home."

The tide has come in and the waves pound below me. The water will continue to rise. It will undermine the pilings and wash them away, lift the room and carry it out to sea.

6. The business card of George F. Berger, M.D., a

psychiatrist and, he told me, a world traveller, whom I met while watching schoolboys playing soccer one evening on the *heden* bordered by the leafy Nya Allen in Göteborg. On the back of his card I have written: "Lions, Early Spring, Men's Locker Rooms"—notes, I imagine, of a bad dream, otherwise unrecorded and forgotten. I never went to visit Dr. Berger, as he suggested after I entertained him by relating a dream or two: scary ones about world leaders and wild animals. I would feel inferior in the presence of a professional man who audibly sucks Clorets. Last night I made a list: I have slept in thirty-one states and nine foreign countries and their tropical possessions with seventy-four women and two men of most of the common races, religions, and philosophies, East and West; more bad dreams and vacant afternoons when it certainly looked like rain.

I am in deep water and it is pouring. The room lists badly, but we are not taking much water; the seams are sound. Out of the windows I can see the dark, steep swells and the land made indefinite by rain and distance. I must have sent Margaret's and the children's stuff on to Providence, for the room is bare, save for these bitter and admonitory scraps in front of me and five apples in the refrigerator, each with a bite taken out of it. Now what does that mean?

What meagre gleanings! It is going to be an immense and unsatisfactory voyage, and already I have used most of them up.

7. A blood-bank card. "SHOW THIS CARD TO HOSPITAL AUTHORITIES IMMEDIATELY UPON ADMITTANCE." Will someone show it for me if I am unconscious? My "CERTIFICATE OF SERVICE IN THE ARMED FORCES OF THE UNITED STATES. SIGNATURE OF INDIVIDUAL." Here I am, and there I have signed with grace. "IF FOUND, DROP IN MAILBOX. POSTMASTER: POSTAGE GUARANTEED." A 1963 calendar from the East Side Savings Bank with most of the days crossed off.

The window is open and things from the sea are washing in. A squid. A small fish with enormous eyes. I have read that in some fish the eyes keep growing larger and larger although the body may be stunted. To what purpose? Here comes a flying fish, sailing into the refrigerator, caroming off and swiftly perishing at my feet. I am in the tropics.

8. My operator's license. "APPLICANT MUST RECORD ALL CONVICTIONS FOR TRAFFIC VIOLATIONS WITHIN PAST EIGHTEEN MONTHS (EXCEPT PARKING)." That's not really fair, officer, for I never park. I'm not turning you on, sir. I keep moving at a speed three miles per hour under the legal limit except in built-up areas, where I travel at a slower rate. I watch out for innocent children and guilty old ladies, do not talk, even to myself, in hospital zones, and turn my radio off when they are blasting. A ticket from a Chinese laundry. "NOT RESPONSIBLE IN CASE OF FIRE OR GOODS LEFT OVER 30 DAYS OR FOR COLORS THAT FADE OR IF TICKET IS

LOST." No fear, Mr. Lum, I have memorized it. My number is J447, my color is white, my mark is R 27, and I have so many distinguishing scars and moles. Paper money smelling of the interior of a dozen women's purses. A card from the YMCA. "THIS IS TO CERTIFY THAT AS OF 9/15/60 INSURANCE, PROVIDING ACCIDENTAL DEATH, DISMEMBERMENT AND LOSS OF SIGHT BENEFITS . . ."

Someone is trying to get in. I go to the door and pull it open. It is Margaret, Patsy, and Mike standing in the rain with paper bags.

"I have a present for you," says Patsy and dumps a number of penny candies on the table. "This is chocolate money," she tells me. "And this is a grasshopper sour and this is an inky dinky and these are buttons and this is a squirrel and this is a zebra."

I am overwhelmed. "Which is the best?" I ask.

"All of them," she says.

"And I have a little present for you, too," says Mike. "It costed me fifty cents." He takes out of his bag one of those puzzles that have lately seemed to me to fairly approximate life as I have lived it. They are shallow boxes covered with glass. Within are a quantity of steel balls, and the object is to jiggle and tilt the box until all the balls have come to rest in a comparable number of depressions laid out in correspondence with one illustration or another—in Mike's gift the joints of a sort of dancing harlequin. There were also, in this case, holes for two of the balls at either end of the dancer's bow tie, evidently intended to represent small bulbs. It generally happens that when you have only one or two free balls remaining, a too violent or abrupt shake knocks all of them loose, and you must begin over again, with less hope of success than before. Moreover, some people's lives, I feel, are broadly illuminated from time to time by what amounts to flashes of lightning. What was dark then becomes visible, revealing the design, and for a moment they no longer have to grope along. Mine, however, has been lighted by something more like the comic or fretful glimmerings of an electrified bow tie, and who will show me the way and the gates?

"And what did you bring me?" I ask Margaret.

"A sea heart," she says.

A sea heart! What could it look like, the heart of the roaring sea? It is, I find, smooth and dark, about the size and shape of a chestnut. Perhaps it had petrified or shrunk—so small and such great labor!—but I cannot conceal my incomprehension and dismay.

"I think you'll find it valuable for holding in your pocket when you're depressed," says Patsy, seeing my look.

"If I were you, I'd rub it against your nose and make it shiny," says Mike, hopefully.

"Don't you like it?" asks Margaret.

It's not a question of liking, is it? More of understanding, the way I see it. But as I've said, they don't know the sea or, indeed, its borders or even, when one follows the rivers back, the famous mountains where the *Auerhahn* courts death; its senses are so dulled by its mating call that the hunter is able to approach. "They call this a sea heart?" I say, stalling. The room has become upright and stationary, and I see through the open door that the sea has carried me back to the land.

"That's what the old man in the shell store said," says Margaret. "I bumped into the kids downtown and we went to the movies. They have matinées when it rains. What have you been doing?"

"Cleaning out my wallet," I say. "I'm a sensational wallet cleaner."

"Don't you want to know what it is?" Margaret asks.

"What what is?"

"A sea heart."

"You are going to destroy my illusions," I say.

"'Sea hearts,' and I quote," says Margaret, "'are the seeds of leguminous trees that grow, among other places, on the west coast of Africa. The currents bear the seeds across the Atlantic and, in time, one finds them on beaches in the Bahamas, for instance,' but I don't believe it for a moment, do you? I think they make them in basements in Miami. What's the matter with you? Don't you like it? Isn't it what you always wanted out of life?"

I review my horoscope (Scorpio) for today: "To forget self and do for others makes this a blessed day for you. Others will be inspired. You begin a chain reaction for good that brings fine benefits in the long run."

"Ma, now he looks kind of lighthearted to me," Mike says.

"I think he's smiling," Patsy says.

"It's hard to tell, though, with his gigantic lips," says Mike.

It is a blessed day. There is nothing, after all, the matter with me, but it is, I feel, a good opportunity for an object lesson. I had taught the children what an object lesson was this way: I pretended to hit them in the face, but when my fist was a half-inch away I held fire and kissed them instead. "You see," I told them, "the object of this lesson is that you never quite know how things are going to turn out. It may look like one thing is going to happen and then another thing does, even at the last moment. So, keep cool or, when playing no trumps, children, always open with the fourth highest from your longest and strongest, and there may come a time when you will be asked to take two and hit to right—in this instance, I recommend you follow instructions." I have always been much better at beginnings than endings, at descriptive passages rather than morals. And, naturally, I failed to get my point across, for they thought an object lesson was to pretend to hit someone and then to kiss them, and that's another thing we do in this rainy weather, pull our punches and smooch.

"I'll tell you what's the matter," I say. "There's a goddam Cheerio on the bath mat. I don't know how it got there and I don't want to, but it's been there for days and no one has picked it up."

I have heard since that Chooch and his roommate won't be building after all. The property and rights were misrepresented, and they have cancelled the deal. In years to come who will wonder why there are bluebells blooming in the valley and marvel at what providence arranged for the flowering peach?

Hello! Goodbye! I Love You!

When my wife left me, I bought a bird for company. I chose a bird over other creatures because I didn't want something around to which in time I would become devoted; it has been my experience that most pets fall mysteriously ill, become melancholy and droop or pine or, inexplicably, run, crawl, or fly away. Besides, my anticipated life span is half over, and I will undoubtedly survive any small animal except for tortoises, parrots, or carp, which are almost everlasting, but toward the end more monument than flesh. There are enough claims made upon me without having to endure these unnecessary impositions of love and death.

Above all, I didn't want a dog. In a way, a dog thinks it is an homunculus, following its master around with a look of imperfect understanding, and how am I to tell it the truth? Furthermore, a dog is bred to be slavish (or to enslave), and I cherish my independence. I didn't buy a fish because I wanted a beast that would be intriguing and talented; fish have their limits. In fact, I wanted a superior kind of bird, one that was clever rather than only pretty or tuneful. We would live together, and if I chose to amuse the bird, or to divert myself with it, that was my privilege, and if the bird cared to amuse me, or to divert itself at my expense, that was its privilege, but our relationship wouldn't become unendurable if neither of us was in the mood. Of course, I accepted certain responsibilities when I bought my bird. I contracted to provide food, water, and gravel, to clean the bottom of the cage and the perches, and to cover the cage with a cloth when there was a draft or the nights were cold. I also reserved, however, the right to cover it when I didn't want to be disturbed—to create an artificial night, as it were, and, if that failed and the bird persisted in its attempts to humor me with silly tricks and chatter, to lock the cage up in the hall closet with my umbrellas and galoshes.

The bird I selected for my pet was a mynah bird; I had been told you can teach it to talk and perform. A mynah is a cunning bird, although one with a forked tongue; I have read somewhere that mynahs' tongues are split when they are fledglings so they can articulate, but this may well be a myth.

I have had my mynah for two weeks now, and have had no success in teaching it to speak even the most rudimentary words and phrases, although I often address it. In the beginning, I tried to train it to say "hello"—a sensible enough start—but for all my pains it only sat on its perch and looked, I thought, scornfully at me. Then I sought to teach it to say "goodbye"—a logical step—but with the same lack of success. I even tried to get it to enunciate a simple, declarative sentence—"I love you;" I failed in that effort, too. I became, as you can imagine, enraged and discouraged. Finally, I gave up. Either I was a miserable teacher, or, more plausibly, my bird had to get acclimated to me, my room, and my way of life before it would respond to my instruction, or you can't teach an old mynah bird new tricks, or, *enfin*, I had a dumb bird.

Two days ago, my mynah made its first sound—a low and variable whistle. It was not the natural whistle of a bird, but a wolf whistle. I have never whistled that way; in fact I think that kind of whistle is common, so the bird couldn't have picked it up from me. Perhaps my mynah is a second-hand bird, and learned to whistle from its previous owner. Thinking the time was ripe, I at once began to declaim its curriculum: "Hello! Goodbye! I love you!" My mynah only whistled in return.

Yesterday, the bird began to imitate traffic noises. No doubt its former owner—for I am now convinced it is a used bird—hung its cage by a window overlooking the street, and it became accustomed to the sounds of traffic. Again I went to its cage and said, with precision and feeling: "Hello! Goodbye! I love you!" My bird merely shifted gears and accelerated in reply.

An hour ago, as I was waching television, I heard my wife say: "I may be mean on the outside, but you're selfish and hide your meanness." So she had thought it over, had returned and let herself in (she never gave back her key, of course), and had decided to make up—on her terms; this spiteful lie was her idea of an overture of peace, which is not unlike her. I turned around, but there was no one besides myself in my room. While I was trying to figure it out, I heard my wife start to say the same thing all over again: "I may be mean on the outside, but you're selfish and hide your meanness." This time I was ready, and whirled about to confront her before she had completed the sentence. It was my bird talking in my wife's voice. As I stared, bewildered and outraged, at the mynah, it started to repeat the inane refrain once more, so I covered its cage. This had no effect; the bird wouldn't shut up.

I have locked the mynah away now, but I can still hear that absurd judgment through my closet door. I have tried to puzzle out this unusual happening, and there seem to me to be several possible solutions.

It could be that my wife had a lover, though I find

it hard to believe she left me for another. But if she did, might it not be, by some terrible coincidence, that my bird once belonged to this man and that she had spoken the sentence to him as she had spoken it to me, and the bird overheard it and memorized it? If my wife and this lover had run off together, then he would not want to be encumbered with a bird. But why should she leave me for him if her opinion of us is identical? Perhaps she was just relating, for her lover's amusement or edification, something derogatory (and inaccurate) about me. This, too, is not unlike her.

However, another equally credible solution presents itself. A mynah bird faithfully reproduces mechanical noises, but I gather that though it can mimic accent and inflection, its timbre is invariable, like the speech of a ventriloquist's dummy or a voice over the telephone. It could be then that the bird's previous owner—a stranger—made the same assertion to his or her spouse, or lover. If there is one such instance, there are, no doubt, others; human relationships, I have always thought, are pretty much on a low level, and overwhelmingly repetitive.

Or, on the other hand, perhaps I repeated this lie in my sleep and that's how the bird learned it; or, even, it's barely possible that the reverberations, the sound waves set off by it had not entirely died out, but lingered, terribly diminished, in my room—for it was, I believe, the last thing that she said to me—and the mynah, having superior or more sensitive hearing than man (here I am not in possession of the facts, and am conjecturing) had distinguished the faint tremors of the syllables.

It may be, too, that a few days ago, when I was passionately seeking to educate the bird, and lost my temper, I inadvertently told it off in those fateful and remembered words. But I must admit a final solution —was the sentence, after all, one that I created and delivered? Was it I who accused my wife so forcefully at the moment of her leave-taking, and have come to attribute the allegation to her; and, when I was vexed with the bird, said it once more? This has to be the reasonable explanation, but it is the one, of course, that I least prefer.

Why, though, did the mynah commit that particular remark to memory? That's the real mystery, for it is not one, you will agree, that is inherently noteworthy.

I suppose I will have to get rid of my bird now, too, and—*quel dommage!*—I had grown rather fond of it.

Them Apples

As Walter Hewlett was gently lowering an egg on a tablespoon into a saucepan of boiling water, his step-daughter skipped into the kitchen with the Christmas cards. Prior to this intrusion, Hewlett had been meditating on the egg. Its shell was blotchy and imperfectly made; it was covered, in part, with minute granules. These irregularities reminded Hewlett of certain sea-shells which are so engrossed by calcareous accretions that they appear monstrous or revisionary. He imagined the egg was not a chicken's but had been wantonly laid by some large, restless sea bird. This speculation did not provoke disgust; it filled Hewlett with a welcome vision of wild, wet, and bitter places where, toward nightfall, the earth's shadow is cast upon the air.

Hewlett felt that his home, like the water's edge, held life's orderly source and surge. At his back he knew that the fronds of his fern were irresistibly uncoiling, that bright, new leaves were ascending from his potted palm, that the light of morning flashing upon their glass hid his prints of flatfish, and their beguiling captions—"*Pleuronectes Passer*, *Der Lincke Stachelflunder*, *Le Moineau de Mer;*" "*Pleuronectes Solea*, *Die Zunge*, *La Sole*, *The Sole*"—as effectively as the lees of the sea, that some sympathetic vibration might suddenly set the strings of his piano thrumming with celebratory music, and that the radiators sang like the tides.

"Walter," said Hewlett's stepdaughter, "did you know that I've had the same dream five nights in a row?"

"No, I didn't, sweetheart. What's it about?"

"I can fly!"

Hewlett saw her suspended and rejoicing above the rooftree.

"This one was sent by mistake to your old apartment on Lexington Avenue," she said, examining an envelope. "Now, *whom* do we know in Miami?"

"Give me that," Hewlett said, grabbing it out of her hand.

"May Good Health, Good Friends, and Happiness be with you for this Holiday Season," the card read. It was signed "Blake." Beneath the signature was written, "Hi there. Member me?"

Hewlett had met Carla Blake in an art-movie house on the Dixie Highway a couple of months before he had been introduced to his wife, now heedlessly sleeping beneath a rose comforter while her old canary tried to wake her with its invariable song. Hewlett had known Blake for a weekend. He saw her now in her bedroom, dark even at midday because of the mango tree outside her window, indolently addressing Christmas cards to all the people she had ever known. Hewlett imagined she could sense his reaction to the card; a filament joined it to a web whose center she held in her hands, and this was the reason she had sent it to him, sent them to everyone.

"Who is Blake?" Hewlett's stepdaughter asked.

"Someone I used to know."

"Does Ma know him?"

"I don't think so," Hewlett said, wondering whether he could destroy the card now that his stepdaughter had seen it.

"This one's from San Francisco."

"It's from Harry and Elaine," Hewlett said.

"Who are Harry and Elaine?"

"Elaine is someone I used to know."

"You used to know an awful lot of people, Walter.

It just says 'Harry.' Do you think Elaine has perished or something?"

"Don't you think it's a pretty card?" Hewlett asked.

"I personally think the Three Wise Men are getting to be a drag this year. No one has any originality anymore. Look, Walter, here's another card from San Francisco—'O-pen your GOL-den Gate.' This one's from Elaine. She says, 'Guess what? Harry and I are getting divorced. How do you like them apples?' "

Hewlett felt threatened and vulnerable, as though Furies whom he thought had abandoned the chase were back on his trail. He remembered, with an intolerable pang, Elaine naked, walking with her odd sailor's gait down the long corridor in her apartment on Russian Hill, which was hung with colored plates from "The Life of the Bee"—"In the Heart of the Flower," "Founding the City," "The Duel of the Queens"—to get him a glass of water in the middle of the night.

"What does that mean?" his stepdaughter asked.

"What does *what* mean?"

" 'Them apples.' It's not even very good English. 'Member me?' Didn't your friends go to college?"

"It means you're a precious little sneak, that's what it means!" Hewlett shouted. "Why the hell don't you mind your own god-damned business? You're always sticking your nose in other people's affairs. You're interested in everything around here except when it concerns you. I'm sick and tired of it, do you hear me? I don't know how you got away with it before I married

Ma, but, let me tell you, there's going to be some goddamned changes around here."

Hewlett watched her eyes brim with uncomprehending tears as though he were looking at a stranger's affliction, or the victim of an accident. She had a small sty on her right eyelid, and what was that pink junk? Chronic conjunctivitis? Gazing over her head, Hewlett noticed that several of the fern's pinnae were yellow, and that his palm was drooping. Did he give them too much water or too little? How the hell could you ever tell? Would the profusion of steam in the morning, and the cold nights, ultimately destroy them? He recalled that the F below middle C didn't sound, and some low note, too, that never appeared in the simple music he played. A mouse—or was it a rat, or a squirrel, or a great, rustling snake?—did something desperately in the walls at night. The exterminator had told Hewlett's wife that it had probably been trapped there when the house was renovated, and since there was no hole, whatever was in there would perish (his word, too) in time and there was nothing anyone could do but wait. Indeed, the mysterious and plaintive noises had become more widely spaced and fainter.

Didn't dreams of flight mean sexual excitement? How old was she? Eleven? My God, my egg!

"I'm really sorry, sweetheart," Hewlett said, holding out his hands to her. "I'm awfully sorry. I didn't mean it. I swear to God I didn't mean it. I promise I'll never do it again. Forgive me."

1109 Klingenstein

Howard Lesser knew that if he finally reached his father's bedside it would be like this, a scene by David, full of tricky light and ardent gestures: His father, always an admirer of views, would tell him to look out of the window—he is not actually a patient, you see, but a guide disguised, Howard not his visitor but on a tour of the hospital. Below, Howard would see a dull portion of Central Park at nightfall. "I used to take you sledding right there when you were a good deal younger," his father would say. His mother would be boiling water for tea with an immersion heater; she had taken the crosstown bus, tangerines and tea bags in her pocketbook. "Do you remember?" she would ask. "Yes," Howard would say, but he wouldn't, for it was other slopes. Why must his father endow the scenery with an imaginary benevolence? He had not, after all, forsaken him. He taught him to sit up at the table, to use the dictionary freely, to save the useful cardboards that came with laundered shirts, to dry his palm on his trousers pocket before shaking hands; and, if you had nothing complimentary to say about your fellow man, to keep silent.

Howard saw himself pretending to be enjoying the view; he would be searching for his father's reflection in the dark panes. He would find him smiling at the recollection of Sundays in the snow. Then, as Howard watches, the smile fades, and is replaced by a look of horror. He has discovered that he was mistaken, that he had never taken his son belly-whopping on that hill, and that his son is aware of this. Howard observes him looking quickly at his wife to see if she has noticed his change of expression, but Mother is intently dipping the tea bag in the cup, as though sounding a familiar but changeful passage. Howard desperately seeks the image of his father's eyes. For a moment, meeting, their eyes seem to share a covert glance of love and admission. "Dad likes his tea weak," his mother says, addressing the ignorant and invisible stranger who always attends her. Howard recoils at his mother's performance. Then he will see, as she turns toward the window, that his mother is weeping. So they all know his father is dying.

"Do you know," his father would say, averting his face as he squeezes the lemon into his tea, "that last night, while I was chatting on the telephone with Sidney, I heard very faintly, in the background, as it were, a fellow presiding over what must have been a bingo game. I could distinctly hear him saying, 'B-fourteen. One-four. G-fifty. Five-O.' And so forth. The damnedest thing. 'Does anyone have a winner?' he kept repeating. How do you imagine that happened?"

"Sid was up to see Dad just before you came," his mother says hopefully. "He's been one of Dad's most loyal friends and greatest admirers down through the years."

"Sidney's a grand guy," his father says. "Not only is he a first-rate dentist but he is a wonderful human being." He speaks as though he is composing an epitaph. "Sidney heard him, too."

"Heard who?" his mother asks, smiling at the unseen stranger, attempting, by the force of her smile, its overwhelming sweetness, to modify or enfeeble her husband's inevitable reply.

"That fellow on the phone I was telling you about only a moment ago, Mother. I called Sidney's attention to him and we listened together. A great many numbers were called, but as far as we could tell, Sidney and I, no winner came forth."

As Howard Lesser, completing the first stage of his reluctant pilgrimage to his father's private room, walked through the Los Angeles International Airport, the willed illusion of a partial face—closer, larger, and more rapt than any lover's—loomed over the apparition of his own. He beheld a noble and venerable ear, irradiated by sunlight, and beyond it—almost, in fact, *through* it, as if it were stained glass—the memory of an idle lady, now, of course, dead, at a window high in a residential hotel on the other side of Broadway, watching him, year in and year out, having his teeth filled. By rights, the hovering face should have been the dentist's, Uncle Sidney's, but it was his father's, its intimacy without purpose and oppressive—hadn't he long ago ceased trying to solve the mystery of their estrangement? Lesser had confused Sidney with his father before. He recalled, feeling as abashed as he had at the time, thanking Uncle Sidney (rushing over to him!) for the gift of a dog—his father had always told him to express gratitude. He had come home and found the unaccountable dog, his father, and Sidney in the living room. Had he embraced his knees? Although he didn't know why Sidney would give him a dog, he knew that his father wouldn't. He was mistaken. Sidney had laughed, but, Lesser realized now, *he* had given Sidney a gift he had no right to bestow, and by that donation had irremediably altered, to one degree or another, the relationship between his father and his father's best—or was it oldest?—friend. Why had he thought Sidney had done it? Sidney was his dentist, a partial face, a classmate of his father's at Townsend Harris Hall, and since he almost always paid his sudden visits after Howard had gone to bed, Howard would only learn by overhearing his parents in the morning that Sidney had been there at all, had stayed a short while, restless and embarrassed, and abruptly left—and that there was, evermore, trouble in Sidney's home. However, Lesser reflected, if he had been unfair to Sidney, Sidney, by his ambiguous presence in the living room that afternoon, had unjustly trapped him, too, so they were equally blameworthy, and his father became their joint and haphazard victim.

Even before that episode, at Swan Lake Manor, his aunt's boarding house in the mountains (the house and the locust trees that obscured it all burned to the ground now; the insurance money swindled from his aunt; she, too, gone now herself), he had raced to his mother across its lawns, then drifted with the locusts' sweet blossoms, shouting, "Daddy's coming! Daddy's coming!"

"Daddy's coming?" she said, bewildered. Howard had admitted that although there was a father arriving from the city, it wasn't his but a playmate's, a father he had not previously met and now no longer remembered meeting, and he burned, then and now, with shame.

Will their positions be reversed, Lesser wondered; will it be, instead, the aimless son who will be looming above the father, over the soundless mouth of the ear's dark, involved tunnel?

On the concourse, Lesser unenthusiastically followed the arrows to Baggage Claim, his raincoat draped over his left shoulder like the blanket roll of a private soldier in some obscure and indecisive war a century or two ago, but his passage was not regulated or emboldened by a regimental band or even the faint measure of a fife and drum; he was accompanied by a string orchestra, whose recorded and lamentable strains flowed from loudspeakers, and he was conspicuously out of step. Indeed, his progress was uneven and regretful, as it had been when he had returned to his play through the fallen blossoms, a ghostly woodpecker drumming on what was soon to become the black ghost of a locust, or when he had turned hopelessly in the living room (Sidney laughing) toward his father.

As he went, Lesser sang nearly under his breath, and to whatever tune was being broadcast, "1109 Klingenstein. 1109 Klingenstein." The night before, in Honolulu, he had received a cable: "DAD UNDERGOING EXPLORATORY SURGERY. ROOM 1109 KLINGENSTEIN, MOUNT SINAI. PLEASE COME HOME. LOVE, MOTHER."

He had dutifully got the 8:15 A.M. jet and was in Los Angeles at 3:15. Lesser had once made the crossing, in the opposite direction, in a small boat. Looking down at the unremarkable sea, he had tried to recall that tedious voyage, but, he discovered, it could only be reconstructed in dreams, where whales broached and bitterly sighed in the dark. What did his father dream about? Lesser imagined his dreams were peopled with allegorical figures in cheap robes who made speeches.

How many times, Lesser thought, have I gone through this airport, the old one before this one was built, other dim and reverberant terminals, with the same hesitant, apprehensive tread, retracing, as upon those two upheaving afternoons long ago, my heedless, departing steps?

The goal was always Baggage Claim, where he would await, without anticipation, the arrival of his familiar and unwelcome belongings. The adjustable razor (grown quite green now) set forever, and arbitrarily, at "7;" his worn and favorite tie, which displayed a pattern of naked boys holding hands (for Gemini); his bathing suit, faded by more than seven seas; "The Case of the Shapely Shadow" and "The Case of the Runaway Corpse": If they were missing, could he begin all over again, run yet another time across distant lawns where spiders hung—swum upon the air!—below the locusts (but what would he cry now?) and, without error, go to his own father in a lost living room?

After he claimed his suitcases, Lesser rented a car and drove out Sepulveda. If he took the next plane to New York, he would arrive when visiting hours were over. He would leave later on that night and get there in the morning.

Lesser knew a girl in Manhattan Beach, which was his destination. He had met her in the Outer Islands, after having got a glimpse of her thighs when she danced on a piano bar. She had told him that she once tried to swim the Molokai Channel in a sharkproof cage; she had snapshots in an album showing her setting forth at night, on account of the tides, the shore operatically lit by torches. There were also several pictures in her collection of a large, powerful man standing on his head on a beach, sipping Lucky Lager through a straw. The girl said he played defensive end for the Rams. "Ha! Ha!" was indiscriminately written, in her hand, in white ink beneath the photographs of the football player and of her unsuccessful and gallant swim.

She lived, when Lesser last saw her—which was more than a year ago—on one of the steep side streets by the Pacific. There was no sign of life when he rang her doorbell. He tried looking in the windows, but the blinds were drawn. Lesser walked down to the beach. There was a cold wind, it was almost dark, and he could smell the oil in the sea. Beyond the breakers, a few boys wearing rubber suits sat patiently on their surfboards in the incantatory light like saboteurs. After a while, Lesser climbed back to her apartment, but again his ring was unanswered. He remembered a high white chest that stood inside her door. It was ornamented with many carvings—Chinese scenes. Lesser regretted that he had never troubled to find out exactly what all the tiny Chinamen were up to. Her bedroom was full of stuffed animals from night-club checkrooms: kittens and pandas, rabbits, tigers, and giraffes—mute and peaceable, as though they had senselessly taken refuge there from a fire or a flood. He had once made love to her on her bathroom sink, staring reflectively past her ear at his portrait in the medicine-cabinet mirror.

Suppose she was hiding in there with one (or more) sulky Mexican bantamweights—or perhaps she had moved, her animals packed in cartons from Food Giant. Lesser tried to picture his father and a strange woman, with a nasty bellhop carrying a suitcase full of bricks or lawbooks and a fifth of Four Roses, slowly ascending in an openwork elevator to a room with a view of the Palisades, and succeeded only novelistically. He thought of writing the girl a note, but what could he say? Lesser had been wholly impelled and made impatient by lust and curiosity—with how many others, in what different rooms? (in Miami, while inexplicable monkeys swung in the tangerine trees; in Cannes, as a dance band played beneath a balcony; in the Tuamotus!)—and all that came to mind to leave her was "Ha! Ha!"

When, at last, Lesser called the airlines, he found to his relief that he could not get a seat until morning. He called Mount Sinai and asked for 1109 Klingenstein. The operator told him that the room did not answer and asked him whom he was trying to reach. Lesser hung up before she had completed her question. Would there be a record of his call? He drove to a motel near the airport and, lying along one edge of a triple bed as though it was also occupied by restless strangers who might suddenly and violently awake, he read a mystery until he fell asleep.

He dreamed he was choking his unconceived child. The boy was about eight and wore Lesser's old wool helmet. Outside the narrow window, the sky was red and full of snow. The paper bag that contained his son's school lunch lay on the floor where he had dropped it in his fright. Lesser awoke, terrified and ashamed. "God protect me!" he cried in the splendid room.

He searched for the girl in the phone book, but she wasn't there; she had vanished, like her contemporaries from the directories of other cities. He called Mount Sinai. The operator told him that it was too late to ring the private rooms. Combing his hair, Lesser left the room.

He stood at the top of the flight of three stairs that led down into the motel's cocktail lounge. It was exceptionally dark, and empty save for three men sitting at the oval bar, each separated from the other by two vacant stools, as though some kind of complicated party game were about to begin. In the center of the bar, a middle-aged lady was playing a small electric organ. The three men were singing an interminable and vastly sentimental college song, an alma mater, and they knew all the words. The years, Lesser gathered, were shining and no one was pining for days gone by, for all their tomorrows would be free of sorrows and sighs. The organist was accompanying them with difficulty, as if she, as well as Lesser, had never heard the song before. At one point in their recital, the three men got off their stools and stood, their hands over their hearts. Every so often, the great whine of a departing jet penetrated the cocktail lounge and threatened to drown them out, but they raised their voices, which were surprisingly true, so that by the end of the song they were singing with incredible force. Lesser saw that they were older than he had realized—really three old men whose collars were too large, whose lapels were too wide, fettered together by an ancient and common chain like galley slaves, and on the verge of tears. He had a feeling that the college in the song was no longer in existence, that it had been torn down for a shopping center or a new subdivision.

As he stood on the brink of the cocktail lounge, Lesser thought he had never seen a more dismal picture, and he turned away in embarrassment. Had his father ever awakened like these old men, like himself, in a motel room, unable to bear or fathom the impositions of loss, deferment, and surrender, and been forced to give a mawkish recital in the dark? No: his father had exemplified, freely declaimed the natural virtues—Prudence! Justice! Temperance! Fortitude!

Lesser had a fleeting vision of the girl, sick and floundering at night in the Molokai Channel, unable to keep up with her towed cage.

Or, perhaps, Lesser thought, it would be like this: The Young Men's Lyceum would have held their final meeting at his father's bedside. The Lyceum was (it is!) a social and literary club of which his father is one of the founding members. "Twice a year we would have a function," his father would tell him from the high, mechanical bed that is not unlike a throne. "In the winter we would hire a hall for our annual banquet. One of the boys was artistically inclined and he did up the programs for our affairs; each one was different, drawn by hand, and generally comical in theme. In the summer, we would charter a motor launch and cruise upon Long Island Sound. I suppose we would take a picnic lunch along and go ashore at one place or another where it was agreeable. Now, of course, a good many of the boys have got older; most of them have died off. That's what happens with the passage of time. It all deteriorates. Who is left? Bob Weiner, Fritzie, Leo, fellow named Harry Dubrow, an attorney in Miami. He's come up once or twice for funerals."

"The Young Men's Lyceum was of very high purpose," his mother says.

"We used to have some lovely times," his father says.

"You should get together with the boys more often."

"Ah," his father says disparagingly. "You know we haven't met for years now. These days, we only come across one another at funerals. That's the way these things happen. You drift apart. You drift apart. Unfailingly."

"Fritzie came all the way in from Leonia, New Jersey," his mother says.

"You asked the boys to come up, didn't you, Mother?"

"Why . . ." His mother would turn to the anxious stranger as her witness. "Why . . ."

"I remember one of the banquet programs this fellow with the artistic bent rendered in India ink. I can't seem to recall his name. It depicted me bereft, a Valentine's heart . . . For one reason or another, Bernard once showed me, in one of his medical texts, an illustration of a human heart. Bernard was a wonderful physician and a lovely guy. After he died, Mother and I had charge of his effects. He had no family and, curiously, lacked what must have been the courage to get married, although he was engaged upon numerous occasions, generally to waitresses in the dingy neighborhood restaurants where he would eat alone, ordering identical meals. When I would talk to Bernard on the telephone in those days, there would be increasingly frequent periods of silence on his part. I finally learned that he had had one or two mild strokes, which he had concealed, and that one of them had cost him some of the power in his right hand, and the receiver would fall into his lap, although he kept on talking. I suppose it was a matter of pride, or disbelief. At any rate, there were, of course, all of his diplomas on his walls. What do you do with diplomas? Can you throw them away? The human heart that Bernard showed me, years ago now, appeared to me to resemble some great barnacled creature that dwells, or reposes, at the bottom of the sea, feebly contracting, and untrustworthy. I suppose our common salinity—the body's, that is—and the perplexing sea's . . . This Valentine's heart was conventionally cracked, and suspended in one of those gentle, cumulous balloons. . . . I'm lost, Mother."

"Heart."

"I don't get you."

"The annual banquet of the Young Men's Lyceum."

"Ah, heart. In this balloon he had lettered—he was a damned fine letterer, too . . . It was a kind of rebus. The broken heart represented a failure in love, thus I was less her. Get it? Less-her. Lesser. Our name! I said they were on the comical side."

"I thought you'd like to see them all again," his mother would say.

"It was a very decent gesture. His name was Perry Julian!"

"Whose was?"

"The boy who did the programs for our banquets. He had really an extraordinary talent. He got a job with the New York Central System, which was quite unusual for a Jewish boy at that time. He eventually went to work in their Chicago office. We lost track of him over the years. That's sort of a pun, isn't it? I heard he died several years back. He never did a blessed thing with his wonderful talent, Perry Julian, which is a shame, a damned shame, for of all the boys in the Young Men's Lyceum he had the greatest chance to make a name in the world."

Because Lesser had failed to reach him, it didn't mean at all that his father had died. Perhaps, like explorers who had sought the fountain of youth and found only embowered and sulphurous but otherwise undistinguished springs, the surgeons, expecting in effect the dismal swamp, had discovered once again the broad and unexceptionally silty loops or meanders of age; or the operator had rung the wrong room; or the cable had been garbled; or it was intended for someone else. He would call again, but it was too early, and, besides, it would be his turn now to be the object of his father's hopeful and extravagant praise. "You know, Howard," he was bound to say, "Mother and I are both very proud of you and all that you've done. You are a credit to us." Lesser longed not to hear those sentences from the lips of this virtuous and coherent man.

At the Sea-Vue Arms

Early one evening, Howard Lesser looked out of the window of his room on the fourth and top story of the Sea-Vue Arms, a semi-residential hotel in south Miami Beach. He had an eastern exposure, but he was unable to see any part of the green, turbid Atlantic he knew to be two blocks away. Many years ago, when he had stopped at the Sea-Vue Arms with his father, Howard had been greatly disappointed to find that the sea was hidden from their window, and, as he further discovered, from every other window in the hotel as well. But then, neither Florida nor his father had been as he had expected. It had rained, his father had dragged him to the Monkey Jungle and the Musa Isle Indian Village beneath his vast umbrella—for he esteemed guided tours—and Portuguese men-of-war were dying all along the beaches. At night, his father raged at him and then locked himself in the bathroom, where Howard could hear him crying and asking for forgiveness.

When Howard thought about it, which was more frequently now that his father was in his late sixties and always harping on one or another obscure and tedious passage of his life, as though warning an uninformed biographer of pitfalls he might otherwise stumble into, Howard realized that it was at the Sea-Vue Arms that he and his father had begun to grow apart. Perhaps, he reflected, that was why he had returned—coming back, as it were, to the scene of an inexplicable crime in which he had been an inadvertent accomplice—and why he was gratified to find that the hotel was faithful to his early, bewildered, and melancholy memory of it, for, in addition to maintaining its fraudulent prospect, the Sea-Vue Arms, now as then, advertised Pullmanettes, heat, an elevator, and being under new owner-management, and, on its broad veranda, the chairs were still arrayed in three perfect rows, as though, Howard imagined, they had been set up for some sort of show (A *tummler?* A dance team? A harmonica player?) that might at any minute begin in the middle of Collins Avenue. So they would not be late or find that all the places had been taken beforehand, old women wearing rolled stockings and sequined hairnets perpetually occupied the seats alongside their forbearant husbands. Were these guests, Howard wondered, the descendants of those who had been steadfastly saving their seats during his previous visit?

The Sea-Vue Arms was but the most recent of a series of second-rate hotels near the water into whose numerous rooms Howard had withdrawn over the years, wayward and disaffected, to read mysteries, follow the comics, and regard the view. Whether they looked out on the Ohio or the Göta, they made up, connected by hot, insufficiently lit corridors that suggested the possibility of rain, a vast hotel entirely tenanted by himself. In one room, he was repairing tattered lire on the bedspread; in another, scratching the names of old loves on his dusty shoes with a peach pit; in a third, standing on the toilet seat pensively spraying mosquitoes.

From his window at the Sea-Vue Arms, which overlooked a bus stop, Howard could see a sign in a storefront that seemed to have been put there, as on a guidepost, to tell him what lay not too far ahead. It implied an endless succession of days and nights spent, marooned, above lobbies decorated with artificial peonies and illuminated eternally by lamps whose bases were statuettes of wandering minstrels, and it offered an inadequate salvation. The sign read, "READ A MAGAZINE TONIGHT."

Later that night, when Howard was on his way back from the dog track, he passed through an alley overhung with trembling, weeping air-conditioners. He looked up and thought they were cages full of unhappy birds, which suited his fancy. A few minutes afterward, he was sitting at a counter on Washington Avenue drinking root beer, looking for a good thing in the *Daily Racing Form*, and frequently sighing. What kept him and his father irreparably apart, he thought for the hundredth time, was that the pattern of *his* life was fanciful and arbitrary, like the constellations, while his father's was reliably repeated over and over as though it were reproduced on wallpaper.

On the occasions when Howard and his father got together, his father would usher him to the brightest corner of the room as though to get a better look at him, and Howard often had the idea he was being dealt with like an unfinished or otherwise unsatisfactory work of art that his father was endlessly striving to perfect. While speaking to him, usually about the inadequacies of Howard's few, small investments, his father would snip away at the hairs in Howard's ears with the scissors contained in his penknife or pick with a fingernail at a spot on Howard's lapel.

"You ought to keep the future in mind," he would say. "Purchase something of known value. You and your *crapauds!*"

(A year or two later, Howard discovered that "Le

Crapaud," or "The Toad," was the title of a poem his father had learned as a schoolboy. "Of course, there's no connection with toad any longer," his father said. "It's just an old and pernicious habit of mine. The poem, by the way, concerns a little boy who, chancing upon a toad, rains stones down on it. I can only remember the last line, which goes, '*J'étais jeune, j'étais cruel.*'" He recited it with a great deal of sentiment, as though he still recalled his teacher's admonition to use more expression.)

"They were tips Marty gave me," Howard would say.

Marty Goldstein, one of the two Goldstein boys—slight, cheerless, and somewhat elegant bachelors who had gone on Caribbean cruises together every winter except for the year each of them had had his major operation—was a classmate of Howard's father's at City College; Marty worked in a branch office of a large brokerage concern located not far from the Tip Toe Inn, on upper Broadway.

"Marty doesn't know anything about the market," Howard's father would say.

"You're always calling him for advice."

"For restaurants. The Goldstein boys know where to eat. I'd use a little sputum on that, if I were you," his father would say at last, the spot on Howard's lapel and the stocks evidently being of equal importance in his long-range view of things.

Howard's waitress and an old lady who was sitting next to him at the counter began to tell each other their misfortunes. He listened, marvelling.

"First my entire wardrobe, including my fur pieces, which I can't tell you how much my husband paid for them, were stolen out of my T-bird whilst I was parked on Wilshire Boulevard," the waitress said. "Then in Vegas—I'm an entertainer, really; I have an act—this fella rammed into me whilst I was making a perfectly legal turn, and, as you can well imagine, the car was nothing but a total wreck. Prior to that I was on Cloud Twenty-nine."

Howard wondered what sort of act the waitress had. She must have been over fifty and had never been pretty. Perhaps she worked with trained animals or was some kind of mentalist.

"Were you hurt, dear?" the old lady asked.

"*Entre nous*," the waitress said, "my ego was hurt the most. But you should listen to my husband on the phone with the insurance company. I can't tell you what a fabulous negotiator he is."

"My Olds 88 was stolen last week from a parking lot by Lincoln Road, dear," the old lady said. "It was paid for and I had all the extras. Then I got myself this rent car, and here I am driving along Biscayne Boulevard minding my own beeswax when somebody shoots at me with a gun from a passing vehicle."

They stopped talking all of a sudden, and Howard

felt that they were waiting for him to say something. It was as though, without his knowledge, he had been assigned a role and had missed his cue.

"I better not hang around you two," he said hopefully. "I might catch some of your bad luck."

"Bad luck?" the old lady said.

"You should be so lucky," the waitress said. "We could have been killed."

The old lady paid up and left, and the waitress moved down the counter as if she had been floated off by a tide. Howard gathered that the performance was over, and returned to his hotel. Had he delivered the right line, or was he supposed to have said something else so that the ending would come out altogether differently?

In the course of his ambiguous vigils in hotel rooms, Howard Lesser had often resorted to reading the notices that were inconspicuously posted there. For instance, some months ago, when he had stayed at a motel near the Los Angeles International Airport, he had read on the bathroom door:

> Please take notice that the proprietor of this hotel (or boarding house or lodging house) keeps a fireproof safe where money, jewelry, documents, furs, fur coats and fur garments, or other articles of unusual value or small compass may be deposited for safekeeping . . .

Now, finding a similar ominous message in the interior of his closet at the Sea-Vue Arms, Howard was put in mind of his father once more. In the past few months, it seemed that on one errand or another his father was always getting after Howard to accompany him to the vault. There, in one of the rooms provided for depositors, which reminded Howard, perhaps because of a common element of hieratic gloom that suggested the nether world, of a booth in a Chinese restaurant, his father would mysteriously rearrange the contents of his safe-deposit box, sadly dealing them around as though he were about to tell a fortune he knew beforehand to be ill-favored or insignificant. Once in a while, he would unfold a stock certificate, and Howard would catch a glimpse of the vignette with which it was embellished. These generally portrayed tableaux of languid allegorical figures, either draped or partly nude, commemorating such events as Science presenting Steam and Electricity to Commerce and Manufacture, and recalled to Howard their counterparts, the four natural virtues—Prudence! Justice! Temperance! Fortitude!—whom more and more he had come to associate with his father, believing even that they attitudinized in his dreams. When his father was convinced that the problem he had set himself, or that life had given him—whichever it was—was once again insoluble, he would slip a rubber band around each of the bundles he had distributed and replace them in the box. "I have always found it wise to carry a quantity of elastics in my pocket," he would tell Howard. "I recommend that you follow my example, as you can never tell when they might come in handy." Indeed, this lesson, or ones of like exemplariness, often appeared in the end to be the sole purpose of the trips to the vault.

At times, however, they would linger on in those dismal, uninhabitable rooms whose air seemed to promise an inferior eternity, and his father would tell Howard about an old classmate who had just died or was now dying, as astonished and ignorant as a fish out of water. These cases had, of course, become more prevalent and bore increasingly upon his father's mind, but, Howard realized, he had, as usual, a further moral or instructive purpose in relating them. He sought to make his son aware of life's perils—compromise and irresolution, to name two of his favorites: History, a recumbent, chapleted Roman, embraces Youth with one arm while pointing out to sea with the other.

Unable to sleep because of the unintelligible gusts of applause, laughter, and fanfares from the television set in the lobby of the Sea-Vue Arms, Howard recalled the last of his father's underground lectures.

"I was attending a convention in Los Angeles," his father had told him, "when Larry Hirschler, whom I hadn't seen since he left New York the previous August, approached me as I was coming out of a meeting. He had taken the bus in from Garden Grove, where, he told me, he was living with his wife and her mother. Despite the great heat, he was wearing an old Tattersall vest he had owned for ages and a double-breasted suit of a cut I don't believe they make any longer; it is the stock costume of refugees, of hayseeds, of actors for whom there are no longer any parts. Larry Hirschler regarded himself as 'a good dresser;' he wore fresh buttonholes in the days, long past, when he could afford them, and I would sometimes see him, when he thought he was unobserved, inclining his head in order to smell the blossoms. Small of stature to begin with, Larry had shrunk terrifically in the intervening year. His clothes looked like they might have belonged to a larger, more jovial partner with whom he had once performed.

"I had known Larry since we were boys; we met one summer when we both sold refreshments on the twin-screw fliers of the Sandy Hook Route, which plied between Pier 81 and several points on the Jersey shore. The harbor was thronged with excursion steamers and night boats in those days—the Mary Powell that left from the foot of Desbrosses Street, the steel steamer Mandalay with its magnificent dancing deck and orchestral music, the Grand Republic of the Iron Steamboat Company.

'The old, old sea, as one in tears,
Comes murmuring with foamy lips,
And knocking at the vacant piers,
Calls for his long-lost multitude of ships.'

"Although I never particularly cared for Larry Hirschler, the way those things are we still kept in touch and had a sandwich together once in a while. Larry really didn't have a very good mind, and he was overbearing and more than a little pompous. He loaded up his waiting room—he was an optometrist—with a bunch of oil paintings he had gotten in a lot at an auction. They were for the most part, I recall, of foliage and cows.

"When he was nearly sixty, Larry Hirschler married. Her name was Minnie, for Minerva, and she was twenty years his junior. He had met her at a hotel in Loch Sheldrake. She played the bass viol, the xylophone, and the drums in the cocktail lounge, and she was not without talent. Mother and I had always regarded Larry as a confirmed bachelor. He had lived for years with three older sisters on the West Side—spinsters—who, in turn, became bedridden and predeceased him one by one, so that if he was not forever trekking back and forth from the lending library for one, he was continually involved in paying out the meagre, complicated bequests of another.

"A few weeks after his marriage, Larry Hirschler called me up and told me he realized what a terrible mistake he had made but that he was going to make the best of it; he had an unreasonable fear of litigation. Minnie and he took a room in a residential hotel near the Park, and she ran up phenomenal phone bills talking to her mother on the Coast. As he got along in years and as his practice, which never really amounted to anything, declined, Larry would sit for hours in his empty office cracking his knuckles and planning vague coups in commodity-futures contracts, or nap on the couch in the waiting room, surrounded by his dark and faintly august paintings. Knowing his financial position, I was surprised one day to learn that he had rented an apartment on the East Side, which he furnished rather lavishly, and that Minnie's mother was living with them. But long before the lease expired, the money ran out, so they took him back with them to Garden Grove, where they live in furnished rooms on his Social Security and the benefits from a small annuity. Larry told me that although he wanted to sell their furniture, Minnie insisted it be shipped to the Coast and stored. Larry thinks she must be up to something, but he can't figure it out, and I was not able to enlighten him.

"He told me that Minnie's mother followed him about, turning out the lights to conserve the bulbs (the electricity was included in the rent), that Minnie had married him for his money, and that he had no one to talk to. 'They are two monsters,' he said. 'Every morning they ask me whether I want one egg or two. Why don't they just put them down in front of me?' He must have been seventy-three or four, and the point was not that he had taken one wrong turn but that one turn was all that he had taken. I wanted to tell Larry Hirschler that Minnie and her mother were not monsters but only appeared monstrous in his eyes, that he had created them as surely as the sleeper evokes the wild animals—which are as harmless and invisible to others as they are fierce and apparent to him—that pursue and spring at him in his dreams.

"As he left, Larry Hirschler told me that he was not going to be buried in his family plot in Mount Zion; there was no more room. 'I am going to be buried in Garden Grove,' he said, weeping. He begged me to deliver his eulogy, for he said no one knew him as I did. 'I want you to know,' he added at the door, 'that I left you in my will the oil painting that hung above the sofa in my waiting room, the scene where the cattle are taking a siesta in the woods. It's signed, and genuine, and French, and, let me tell you, more than one person has told me that not only is it a work of art but it's worth money. Anyway, I know for a fact that the frame will bring you a good price if you choose to sell.' "

The next morning, as Howard Lesser was on his way to breakfast, one of the old men on the veranda of the Sea-Vue Arms gave up his seat and approached him. "Sonny," he said, "the people were kind enough to tell me you were a Lesser, and I was wondering whether it could be any relation to my old friend. So, close up, I see it is really and truly his son. Your father has frequently spoken glowingly of you to me, sonny. A fine fella, your father. The name's Hirschler, if you hadn't already guessed it. Your father told you all about Hirschler, his best friend? How's he making out?"

"O.K.," Howard said, reflecting that he might very well have guessed Hirschler's identity if he had not been so surprised by his prodigious occurrence, for he was wearing the same getup Howard's father had described; he had added only a waterproof cap, a collection of ball-point pens and mechanical pencils that jutted from his breast pocket, and, in his lapel, a flower that Howard recognized as having come from a shrub in Lummus Park. Howard feared that Hirschler might at any moment withdraw as abruptly as he had appeared, and that he would not have time to fully comprehend the old man's significance; he reminded Howard of a figure who emerges from one of the tiers of the galleries of the automata on antique clocks, performs an enigmatic act, and then retires.

"In the pink," Hirschler said. "That's nice."

"I thought you were living on the Coast," Howard said.

"You call that living?" Hirschler said violently. "Let me tell you something. I got out of that Coast joint pretty goddam quick. I'm in the process of negotiating for a plot in Mount Nebo down here where I feel at home. Perpetual care's included."

"Did you finally make your bundle in the market, Hirschler?" Howard asked.

"I am about to take the plunge with both of my hands

any day now," Hirschler said, "I'm watching it like a hawk, a hawk. You know, my bumping into you here like this brings to mind that right up to this very day I recollect counselling your father about a matter of a terrific plunge he went ahead and made anyway, which, naturally, led to some bath. There was a couple of mining issues—highly speculative propositions, let me add once and for all—that once upon a time were listed on the Toronto Exchange. Do you happen to have any kind of a notion what they are today? I'm going to tell you—a couple of empty holes in the ground. I tried to tout your father off of them, but they had caught ahold of his fancy. What a sensational tumble he took! Afterwards, he listens. I prescribed for him a change of air. Take a little trip to sunny Florida, I told him. I recommended the Arms here. Take the little shaver along with you, I told him. He'll keep your mind off all manner and means of trouble . . ."

As Hirschler went on, Howard noticed that the waitress who had served him the night before was occupying the seat next to the one that Hirschler had just vacated. She must be Minnie, as he might have known, and Howard felt as though he were going once more through a tunnel of love in which he had ridden at a seaside park years before, where clumsy apparitions in need of repair lunged unsucessfully at him in the dark.

"No, it was Minnie's mother kicked off," Hirschler was saying. "She was a monster, believe me when I tell you. You see, sonny, I had three sisters who kicked the bucket before her, and I know all about how to go through effects with both of my hands, sonny, both of my hands. Don't worry, Hirschler's had experience in that line of work, and I know these old bags have cash money that's tucked away, but they don't figure on a Hirschler who knows all about it from way back. I found it pretty goddam quick, and I told my Minnie—what a woman! You'll meet her! Some musical ability, too!—let's get the hell out of this Coast joint."

"But he recouped, didn't he?" Howard said.

"Recouped? Who? Who? Who are you talking about?"

"My father."

"Oh. Oh. It depends on how you want to look at the thing," Hirschler said. "I mean to say, of course he rebounded, but it was a blow at the time and he was short of funds there for a while. He went into gilt-edges later on when he could maneuver a little bit—stuff like that. That wasn't quite what I had in mind for him to buy into, but he was playing a little scared there. He certainly won't be leaving the legacy he would've if he had listened to me in the first place is what I'm trying to get across. Formerly, your father used to be quite a wealthy fella.

"I want you to come up to my room and see something for a minute, sonny," Hirschler went on. "It'll knock both of your eyes out. It'll make your trip to Florida worthwhile, I guarantee it."

Howard went up in the elevator with Hirschler and

followed him down the dim corridor to his room. What imperfect, gibbering illusions, Howard wondered, would pounce at him next? Must life become, he thought, a succession of futile disguises and unmaskings?

"This junk all goes," Hirschler said, indicating the hotel furniture. "Our bedroom suite is being shipped Railway Express from the Coast. However, I brought *this* item along in person."

He pointed to a large painting in a heavy, carved, gilded frame which was propped up against the wall next to a set of pearly drums. It was, no doubt, the painting that Howard's father said Hirschler had willed to him, for it portrayed a number of cows lying in a wood. It was done in the manner of Charles-Émile Jacque, and was almost entirely without merit.

"Look at them leaves on the trees, sonny," Hirschler was saying. "Each one of them's a masterpiece in its own right. Look at them cows' snouts, the way they look so humid, like the article itself. Come here and take a look at this French signature here. That's genuine, sonny—an authentic French name . . ."

Howard was looking out of Hirschler's window, trying once more, the way his father had endlessly brooded over his securities, to find the ocean. It could not be done. Howard supposed that Hirschler's disreputable tidings explained much of what had happened since he and his father had checked into the Sea-Vue

Arms—events that had culminated in the interminable visits to the vault, where, he gathered, his father had wanted to let him know that a great number of the certificates were *crapauds*, that he wouldn't be leaving nearly as much as he had once hoped, and each time he was, at the last moment, unable to confess his one unendurable folly.

At least, it appeared that his father would be saved the trouble of disposing of the painting. It was not at all in his style. He would have preferred, Howard thought, some work of Poussin's, *tableaux vivants* on the order of "La Traversée de la Mer Rouge" or "Moïse Changeant en Serpent la Verge d'Aaron." An engraving made from a Poussin would have been even more fitting, for his father abhorred ostentation; but Howard had heard that the engravers had often attempted to enliven Poussin's figures by putting in eyeballs that the artist had deliberately left out, an alteration and disfigurement that his father would have been sure to detect and disapprove of. Howard learned later that he had been entirely misinformed in the last regard, but this did not seem inappropriate; he reflected that as he grew older it was actually more often the case that whatever fresh insight he gained came not from the introduction of new evidence but from the elimination of former beliefs which proved to be insupportable.

"You know, sonny," Hirschler said, "your father always admired this particular work of art. As a matter of fact, he was a great fancier of it. I was thinking it might make him a suitable gift. Since you're the son, I'm making a special price of only a hundred and seventy-five dollars, which, I don't have to tell you, is a steal."

If, as he supposed, his father's account of Hirschler's intended bequest was accurate, what could Howard reply?

"A hundred and fifty," Hirschler said. "Listen, I'm sacrificing. Sonny, how does a hundred strike you? This is rock bottom."

Ashamed, Howard turned to go.

"Don't leave me, sonny," Hirschler pleaded. "Name your own price. I'm practically on both of my knees. The frame. Don't forget the frame!" Then he added, weeping, "I can't afford my plot."

Howard remembered accompanying his father to *his* father's grave, which lay beyond the end of a subway line. Howard's grandfather, an immigrant, had died penniless and unrewarded, and it was, Howard felt, these conclusions that now oppressively haunted his father. As they approached the plot, clamorous, detestable old men had shuffled toward them from among the headstones where they had been lounging and plucked anxiously at their sleeves. Howard's father told him that these old men were called "firemen," because of the way they came rushing up. His father selected one from the number and he went along with them to the grave, the old man complaining to Howard's father how it hurt him in here and hurt him in there. At the plot, the old man said an *el moley rachamim* and Howard's father gave him two dollars. As they waited on the subway platform for the train that would take them back to the city, Howard's father recited a stanza he was fond of:

"Nor deem the irrevocable Past
As wholly wasted, wholly vain,
If, rising on its wrecks, at last
To something nobler we attain."

Finding Hirschler preposterously bereft in a Pullmanette out of sight of the sea, Howard was reminded anew of his father tormented in the coupon rooms, and he realized that if he revealed to him what he had just learned—was it, after all, to be believed?—and told him he had no need of second-hand money or the impositions of righteousness, that all he wanted was his impure love, it would be as unavailing as if he confronted Hirschler with his knowledge of him; they were set in their truly mysterious ways. Howard wondered whether, on the bright decks of the twin-screw fliers rounding Sandy Hook and bound for Atlantic Highlands, Long Branch, Asbury Park, Belmar, Point Pleasant, they knew how little time was left them before they would become distressed by their unappeasing preoccupations.

In the Tuamotus once, Howard had bathed in an enamelled basin. The *salle de bain* had a curtained door. It was enclosed by corrugated-iron walls that rose above the bather's waist and was open to the sky. It had a gravel floor. A drum of rain water that had been warmed by the sun stood in a corner. Seated in the basin one evening, his knees drawn up, smoking the remaining inch of his cigar, Howard could see only the clear, darkening sky, hear the murmurous pigs by the lagoon's edge, the chickens laying eggs on his flowered-chintz bedspread, and, from the neighboring houses, a piece of piano music being broadcast from Tahiti. He felt then that he had fortuitously achieved a perfect, equilibristic state, one that he could maintain only for this single moment in his life before he fell forever from it. Poised, he heard several great splashes; it was, he knew, the pair of leopard rays that came predictably into the harbor at nightfall, turning and turning again in their devious search like partners in a dance. Their portentous advent made him reaware of the unimaginable shapes that lie ahead like breaching leviathans or the ghostly contrivances in the windings of the tunnel of love. Faintly, he heard against the shore at last the diminishing wavelets engendered by the rays.

"For Christ's sake, Hirschler, sell the bedroom suite," Howard said.

"It was sold, sold, sold years back," Hirschler said.

"Hock the drums then."

"I'm in the process right this very minute," Hirschler said, "of negotiating a sale with a fella down here, who was formerly a prominent drummer in a famous dance band, to take them off of my hands. He's going to call me back."

"I'll tell you what I'll do for you, Hirschler," Howard said. "Give me two dollars."

"Two bucks? He asks me for two bucks! Sonny, I'm a busted valise."

"Fork it over, Hirschler."

Hirschler gave him the two dollars, and Howard recalled once more how the "firemen" had beset him and his father like jackals, how they had had to beat them off.

"What are you going to do with it?" Hirschler asked.

"I'm going to put it on a horse's nose for you, Hirschler," Howard said. He didn't know whether he was trying to buy a little more time or affirming the chance and promise that life endlessly presents.

"You got some information?"

"He'll win laughing."

"Thank you, sonny," Hirschler said.

"Thank *you*, Hirschler," said Howard. "And may he have a speedy journey."

Anna Banana

"What made you wake up?"

"Well, first of all, you see, I was seeing colors in my head. I think I was just dreaming about colors. Then I heard this crashing noise, and I opened my eyes. In a window across the garden there's a red light burning. Then I saw firemen climbing up and down the fire escapes, breaking everybody's windows with big hatchets. At first, I couldn't tell if it was smoke out there or just the regular, natural night. I took one more look and came in your room and got in your bed. It makes it safer. You know, to have someone with you."

"Do you want to talk?"

"I don't care."

"What do you mean you don't care?"

"I mean, I don't care if we do talk and I don't mind if we don't talk."

"Doesn't anything make any difference to you?"

"Maybe I'd feel a little better if we did talk, but it really wouldn't hurt me much if we didn't."

"Do you think we talk enough?"

"What?"

"To each other."

"Yes, even if you're always working, I see you a lot and we talk quite a bit."

"Do you think we're good friends?"

"We're more than friends."

"What are we?"

"Friends that are friends and friendly are more than friends."

"I no capeesh that."

"I'm nine years old. You shouldn't expect too much of me."

"You don't seem very friendly now—here."

"I'm thinking about Anna."

"Anna Banana?"

"I wish you wouldn't always call her that. That's only a little joke we have between us when she comes to baby-sit. Her name is Anna Schiano, and I hope she's all right."

"Why shouldn't she be?"

"She lives over there, you know. She's lived in that same building for sixty-one years. She told me herself."

"Do you wish I would do more things with you?"

"Not really, because you have to work to get money so you can get time off to do things with me. I don't mind waiting. But I hate it when I come into your room while you're working, because you say, 'What do you want?' and I have to say, 'Nothing,' because I know you're going to tell me, 'Get out.' It's not 'nothing.' I just want to be with you."

"What kind of things would you like to do with me someday?"

"Maybe play golf."

"Golf! What do you want to play golf for?"

"Because you said it's interesting."

. . . "Did you think I was sleeping just then?"

"When?"

"A few seconds ago."

"No. When you sleep, your eyelids don't wrinkle up. They hang straight down."

"Do you think I was deliberately pretending to be sleeping?"

"Yes, I think you closed your eyes because you wanted to see if I'd stay awake, to see if I care about people or not. Perhaps someone else would go to sleep if they saw their father go to sleep—say it must be

O.K., I'll go to sleep, too. You were testing my wits."

"Why would I do that?"

"To see if I could take a responsibility."

. . . "You still here?"

"I want to make sure nothing happens. That the fire doesn't come across the garden and creep up the stairs. I was looking for little sparks. Go to sleep. I won't let you down or leave you."

"Did anything happen?"

"Anna came out on the fire escape in her nightie. Two firemen went up and led her down to the garden, and she looked up and saw me and waved. I opened the window and shouted at her to see if she was O.K. She said sure, and not to worry about her."

"Did she know I was here?"

"She asked for you, and I said you were tired from working, and I was watching the house so you could get your sleep."

"You're making this up, aren't you?"

"You want her to be all right, don't you—Anna Banana?"

"I want to know if you're telling me the truth."

"Howard, why do you have to be so boring? . . . Please don't cry. I'm sorry. Kiss me, I'm Irish."

Lesser Married

One night, in the midway of his mortal life, going to Grandma's, his wife, Valerie, seated beside him in the rented car, his two stepchildren in the back singing to their dogs, Howard Lesser realized that once again he had been mistaken. In this instance, it was in regard to the shark-proof cage, made of chicken wire and supported by empty gasoline drums, in which a girl whom he had thought he loved had attempted, unsuccessfully, to swim the Molokai Channel. Over a year ago, Lesser had had a vision of the girl, foundering in the dark, unable to keep up with her towed cage. He was now aware that his revelation had been imperfect, for, in anticipation of this contingency, the cage had been built with only three sides. There was no back to it. If, then, the sharks could enter it, so could she leave, and that had been the case. Lesser recalled her telling him that she had become sick from watching her cage swinging beneath her in the unusually clear water and had at times forsaken it to swim alongside. "But my boatmen were always falling asleep and leaving me behind," she said.

She had told him, too, one night before she fell asleep, of another swim she had undertaken. It had started at midnight in Egypt, on the Great Bitter Lake, and was a race. "The water was terribly warm and salty," she said. "My rowers spoke no English, and I didn't know where we were going, because there was no moon. After a while, I passed another swimmer. Two hours later, I passed him again. I had the feeling I had wasted a lot of time swimming in circles, that I had been misled and had lost my way."

As she slept, Lesser had listened to her breathing, and heard, as though from underwater, the unvarying, organic notes of her exhalations, which had been her accompaniment as she crossed the Great Bitter Lake; the bedclothes at their feet were the vague, conspiratorial rowers, wrapped in their galabias, leading them both astray.

What had happened to her whose head he had so often held between his hands in the dark, looking down into her wholly open eyes, which were, he felt, like stars whose light, though freely present, was not certainly meant for him, coming from so far, but perhaps for the next or the one before?

Lesser wondered about the fortunes of the lost, scattered girls he had known and now, most likely, would never see or hear of again, and he often imagined that they had fallen on hard times. Was it his abandonment that had humbled them, or had he, rather, held their heads abovewater for a while? He reëncountered them in his dreams, unattractively aged or carelessly disguised as himself. They waylaid him in ruined municipal swimming pools full of weeds and leaves; in the lobbies of hotels by harbors where palms and rubber plants grew in Wesson Oil tins, and he could smell the floor of the sea; in the South, in stuccoed pensions overlooking dovecotes from which the doves had long ago flown, or bus stops whose benches bore advertisements for scenic railways and mineral water; at a café in Neuilly where every morning one winter he had composed picture postcards as though they were notes to be set afloat in bottles.

He pictured them as having settled for inferior marriages, or grieving over the death of cats, or, in the case of the long-distance swimmer, living on a tiny, silent concrete court next door to a laundry room in one outlying part of Los Angeles or another, falling behind in the payments on her car, her phone shut off, her begonia unwatered, sitting naked on the floor in front of her television set, weeping. Lesser felt that she, that others of different years and cities, were really the only ones who knew, since he had forgotten, who he had been and was no longer, and what he pined for was not the loss of their love but its object—the slender, uneasy person whom he found looking at himself, proleptically suppliant, in half a dozen snapshots, and barely recognized. In these trivial moments, irrelevantly preserved in the photographs, Lesser seemed to be impatiently waiting for the shutter to fall so that he could resume his steep, sad, anfractuous, and irremeable way.

> "Life is a string of pictures hanging
>   up to dry.
> Who will have my memories?
>   Pretty colors! Buy!"

his father had written inside the cover of the album that contained photographs of his marriage and honeymoon —a motto which Lesser felt hardly exemplified his own wary poses. Lesser and his parents had gone through the album together on the morning of Lesser's marriage. His parents' wedding had taken place in the Catskills, at Swan Lake Manor, on the south lawn, with the local butcher, who was also a rabbi—and, his father said, "looked like pig"—officiating, and four men holding the *huppah* down against the unexpectedly high wind that had arisen during the ceremony. Lesser's mother had carried a bouquet of wild flowers that his father had gathered, bicycling after them early in the morning. The hotel had since burned to the ground and many of the wedding guests who had come up to the mountains en bloc in a parlor car were dead now, as were several of the lounging figures who appeared later in the salons of the S. S. Cape Eternity or on the great, dim porches of the Bay of Naples Inn. As Lesser turned the pages, his father said, referring to this one, "He became a very successful doctor and died young," or to that one, "I don't remember his second name. He worked for a large firm of insurance adjusters at 140 Liberty Street. He died," and, of a first cousin once removed who had spoken at the wedding, "He was a graduate of a St. Petersburg Gymnasium and came to New York in steerage. He stepped ashore wearing a second-hand tuxedo he had purchased in London from an Italian waiter. It was the only suit of clothes he had to his name. He first worked for a concern that manufactured suspenders. Then he became involved in a scheme for shipping salicylic acid, in salts, to Russia, which failed. For a time, he attended the Baron de Hirsch School. The Baron was a German philanthropist who believed the Jews should return to the land. Agriculture didn't suit him. He was widely read, very highly regarded, and an exceptionally soft and gentle human being. Although he never found his métier, he was never dismayed. He told me once, 'There are so many divergent paths to follow, but who has found one that does not converge at the same point as any other?' He died—short, short of his prime—of tuberculosis. I delivered the principal eulogy at his funeral, which was very well attended. He had admirers from all walks of life."

One photograph in the album showed Lesser's mother and father cavorting unaccountably on the beach at Neponsit. "You know that painting of someone and someone fleeing the Garden of Eden" his father said. "Mother and I were probably imitating that."

"It's all coming apart," his mother said. On their laps, looking like ashes, were fragments of the disintegrating pages. "It's simply dreadful. We must do something about it."

"I doubt that we'll ever look at it again," his father said.

"When you see yourself in these photographs, do you remember who you were?" Lesser asked his father.

"I don't," his father said, with no apparent regret.

"I do," his mother said. "I remember exactly who I was. I have always remembered who I was at every minute of my life, just as if each of those minutes were this one."

As Lesser turned off Interstate 84, he was stopped by a policeman who stood in the middle of the road before an underpass, signalling with a flashlight. Stepping on the brakes, Lesser could feel himself beginning to panic. What offense had he committed now? "Pull up behind the others," the policeman said. Others? Lesser saw that just beyond the underpass a number of cars were parked on the shoulder. Somewhat relieved to find there were accomplices, he turned off the ignition and the lights, set the emergency brake, and waited anxiously by the unfamiliar highway.

"What have you done?" his stepson asked.

"I don't know," Lesser said.

"You may proceed now, sir." A different policeman had spoken, startling Lesser, for he had not noticed his approach. The policeman's face bobbed at the window like a distressed swimmer's.

As Lesser drove off, passing the row of parked cars, he tried to make out their still, suspicious occupants. He wanted to see what it was that had set them apart from him and his family, why he had been allowed to go while the others had been detained. What was it about him (or did it have to do, rather, with his wife or the charming presence of dogs and children) that bespoke his innocence, and what incriminated the others whom he had left behind? Lesser had hardly been able to discern them, but they had seemed undistinguished, idle, and indifferent. What was worse, he wondered—to be confronted with an unspecified guilt or with an innocence that was inexplicable?

. . .

Later that night, Lesser lay in a strange, yielding double bed waiting for his wife to finish talking to her mother—Grandma—and one of her mother's old cousins, and come upstairs. The bedroom, which was, Valerie had said, where she and the two youngest of her sisters had slept together for so many years in the bed in which he was now lying, was decorated for the most part with odds and ends that Grandma said she had picked up for a song at auctions. A tinted photograph, a panorama of the front at Charleston, South Carolina, behind which an old palm frond was looped, hung next to a lithograph of a painting of the Madonna and Child by Sichel ("1844–   "). A copy of the "Idylls of the King" was pinioned beneath one foot of the bureau, evidently to make it level. On the bureau top, a calendar painting depicting Christ and the effluent stain of His Sacred Heart was perched in a spray of artificial cherry buds and blossoms, which stood, in turn, in a vase of hobnail milk glass. "I will bless every place where a picture of My Heart shall be set up and honored," was printed beside the illustration; in the lower right-hand corner was an appeal from a Father Ralph, whose mailing address was 316 North Michigan Avenue, Chicago 1, to pray for missionaries in Japan and the Philippines.

The room, Lesser decided, was as inaccessible, essentially, as those in which he imagined his father composing his sentimental diaries—rooms that were utterly gone, with even their space dispersed, for Lesser had situated them on the upper stories of tenements that had long since been torn down, other buildings erected in their place. Valerie had told him that she and her sisters had all been born at home, and Lesser inferred that this was the natal bed, here the original room, the unapproachable tower of the stern, disquieting little girl whom he had seen in the photographs in the albums they had been leafing through before he had come upstairs. Lesser felt that only some inadequate part of him—one hand, swollen, feeble, and clumsy—had gained admittance to the room, was lying on its back on the bed, uncomprehending. The rest of him was outside. His great, dazed head rested on the lawn, his body reached well across the road, his feet were in the dark orchard. Lesser had not been aware of the existence of his father's diaries until the morning of his wedding. He had found them on a high shelf in the disused maid's bathroom, where his father had asked him to put the album of wedding photographs away. Once, he recalled, the bathroom had been steamy, faintly exotic or tropical, and perpetually hung with stockings and underpants. Lesser had only been able to scan the diaries, for the arrival of the first guest had coincided with his discovery. There were ten volumes, bearing the imprint of various stationers and containing tables of weights and measures, obsolete maps, and lists of old lacrosse champions. They spanned the years from the time his father had been at City College until the day he had got married—

chiefly a record, it seemed, of trifles, perplexity, and disappointment. Lesser had copied out one of the entries.

"What is there to write today?" it went. "All that has happened is that I have awaited her call—in vain and in vain. The phone rang once, but it was only Sidney suggesting we 'amble' (as he always puts it) over to the river to see the Pacific fleet. Another day totally wasted! *Eheu fugaces*, etc. Why do I persist in the illusion that she will come back? Yet another folly! It is 'very pitiful and as true.' I am so 'headachey,' depleted, *abattu*. Ah, I rhyme!"

When Lesser envisioned his father writing the diaries, he saw him from the back, bent over a card table, wearing a dark suit he had outgrown. There was a window before him, and through it Lesser could see the ancient, populous city. It lay far below him, the air thickly moted, hot, brown, as though in rotogravure. Lesser waited on the threshold for his father to finish, rise, and turn around. When he did so, Lesser saw that he wore a mask that was an enlargement of the tiny, smiling face that had appeared in the photographs of his wedding; without the cumulative, toppling waves of hair his father had favored at that period it was, unremarkably, like Lesser's own. Lesser knew that Sidney had turned out to be his dentist, but he wanted to ask his father who "she" was, whether she had ever returned and become his mother, or if she had disappeared, but his father walked right by him as though the mask had no peepholes. Lesser felt as though he had crept up to his father while he was sleeping and shamefully read the sorrowful, adumbrating boughs and furrows of his unguarded palm. How many years had it been since he last saw his father asleep, his face folded and aged, expressive of the austere presentiments of his dreams? What did the tender interior of his father's hand look like?

"Valerie, how come you never showed me no pictures of you and Howard's wedding?" Lesser heard the voice of the old cousin through the open register in the floor.

"Valerie, get Marie the snaps in the commode," her mother said.

Lesser got out of bed and lay by the register, looking at the women in the living room below.

"Did I tell you about Joe's Lucille's?" the cousin said. "They held the affair at the Manhattan Hotel, you know. The Olympia ballroom. I hadn't been since it was the Lincoln, so you can tell how often I step out. There was beer and whiskey on every table and we made the toasts with champagne. Here I am dying for a cup of coffee. I kept asking Ang', you know, how can I get my hands on a cup of coffee, I'm dying. There were two bands there that played, one colored, one white, that made music all night. One hundred and forty people showed. My Frank kept asking me to go dancing with him. I dance the Peabody, that's all, I told him. He kept after me, so finally I told him, O. K., but no funny stuff. On the floor, Frank said to me, now you look like my sweetheart. I told him, you're crazy, and to lay off the free whiskey they're handing out, and how about getting me a cup of coffee. I give Lucille a half a hundred. I did it for her sister, too. Thank God, she's the last of them. My usual tops is twenty-five.

"So these are them," the cousin went on. "Whomsoever took them takes a nice candid shot. A small gathering, I see. Very intimate. Valerie, you should have held it in a suite, if you don't mind. Who's that over there kissing you, looks like William Powell from the distance?"

"That's Howard's father," said Valerie's mother. "Howard favors him."

"They both have very distinguished hair," the cousin said. "Who's this little old monkey hanging around in every picture here? Look, everywhere you look he's sticking two cents in."

"That's the horrible man," Valerie said. "He died a week after the wedding in the balcony of Loew's Valencia. Howard's father had known him all of his life and he never cared for him, either. His name was Feuerman. No one invited him. He just showed up."

"There's a lot of nerve," said the cousin.

"Marie, he rings the doorbell right in the middle of the ceremony," Valerie's mother said. "So help me, I was mortified."

"He wouldn't go away," Valerie said. "Everyone could hear him breathing."

"I was only passing by," Feuerman had said when Lesser's father answered the door. "I was in the neighborhood by *pure chance*. You're wearing your *bar-mitzvah* suit."

Lesser's father explained that his son was getting married.

"Some coincidence," Feuerman said.

Lesser's father led him into the living room.

"Going right ahead with what you were doing, everybody," Feuerman said. "Don't mind me for a minute. I'm standing here in the background where no one will notice."

The judge resumed the ceremony. Lesser watched Feuerman's reflection in the pane of glass that protected a studio photograph of his mother done up as a Japanese maiden, which hung behind the judge's head. For some reason, Feuerman had struck a hierophantic pose, letting his prominent eyelids droop. Had he bestowed a blessing or imposed a penance? Lesser knew that the act of marriage could not atone for all his old recklessness and defaults; it was, however, bringing about something else—a forsaking of a kind of perfection or elucidation that he had once sought to attain and that he now realized he would forever fall short of, a vision of which he must at one time have glimpsed from afar, for what else had set him so inconsolably forth?

After the wedding, Feuerman said to Valerie, "You'll meet my wife sometime. She used to be an artiste." Then he said to Lesser and his father, "To make a long story short, I need two hundred and fifty dollars. It's a matter of life and death, I don't have to tell you. It's deductible. A bad debt. No point my kidding you in this day and age."

Lesser's father took Feuerman aside, wrote out a check, and gave it to him.

"I've got to run," Feuerman said. "Say goodbye to everybody for me."

"The way he keeps turning up," Lesser's father said when he had gone. "A pathetic case."

"Who was that dreadful old man?" Lesser's mother asked.

"Don't you remember Harry Feuerman?" Lesser's father said. "For a while, he had a little mill-end business on Lispenard Street. He came to our wedding, too. You'll find him smiling idiotically in the photographs. I remember how he stalked across the south lawn that morning, shouting, 'Dr. Lesser, I'm presuming!' "

"I would never have recognized him in a million years," Lesser's mother said. "He's changed a great deal."

"I expect we have, too," Lesser's father said.

His mother seemed about to protest, but she turned away instead; it was a practiced movement, like an old dance step. Lesser thought how often his father had upheld to him the example of his abiding marriage. It wasn't less than that, but at times he felt his father resembled a beggar who displayed to passersby his artificial leg.

When Lesser and Valerie were waiting in the corridor for the elevator, Lesser looked beyond his mother and father, who stood in the doorway to see them off, into the apartment in which he had just been married. His parents had recently moved upstairs from 3–B, where Lesser had spent his youth, to 11–B, where his mother was fond of pointing out the amplitude of natural light and the panoramic views they had never been able to see from below. The apartment was laid out and furnished exactly like its predecessor, and might well serve, Lesser thought, as the setting for a predictably bad autobiographical play. Indeed, their parts and lines—his mother's, his father's, his own—seemed unchanged, but the actors were all miscast, deficient, and bewildered. Lesser heard a great, almost remorseful whine at the bottom of the shaft; the elevator had started its ascent. He asked his father who was living in 3–B. His father said he didn't have any idea. The elevator doors slid open. "Goodbye," Lesser said to the couple who were struggling to perform the roles of his mother and father. "Goodbye," they said to Lesser, but he had slipped away years ago.

Lesser had met the woman who played the part of his mother the night before. He had slept once more in his old bed; he wanted to be on hand early to help out with the wedding preparations. In the middle of the night, he had got up and gone into the living room. She had followed him there, turning on lamps.

"You shouldn't sit in the dark," she said.

Lesser saw an elderly, somewhat haggard stranger holding his mother's familiar robe about her; she kept glancing about with ingratiating smiles, as though she were attempting to ascertain where the audience was sitting.

"I heard you moving around," she said. "I thought something might be the matter."

"Go to bed," Lesser said.

"I wasn't sleeping anyway," she said, holding her ground. "I'll get you a glass of milk."

"I don't want anything," he said.

"I don't sleep much anymore," the woman said.

Lesser went back to bed. He heard her wandering around the apartment. He must have let her down somehow, too, he gathered.

"Who's that nice-looking young fella there?" the cousin asked. Through the grate, Lesser could see her pointing to a loose snapshot. Valerie, her mother, and the cousin were seated on a green plush couch, which had several buttons missing, looking as though they might be making a railway journey. The wedding pictures were strewn about their feet.

"That's Eddie Quinlan," Valerie's mother said.

"I never heard of him," the cousin said.

"Valerie was sweet on him once upon a time," her mother said. "Valerie, by the way, I didn't tell you—he called up."

"When?" Valerie asked.

"Two years ago."

"Why didn't you let me know?"

"I didn't see any reason to," her mother said. "I didn't let on you were divorced or anything, let me tell you."

"How did he sound?"

"He sounded fine. He wanted to know how you were and what you were up to. Like that. I told him you were fine. Why not? There was no point going into everything, was there? We had our little chat and we hung up, and that was that."

"What's happened to him?"

"He said he was working for one of those big airplane companies out there in California."

"Had he gotten married?"

"The subject didn't come up in our conversation. What difference does it make now?"

"You should have told me, Ma."

"God is my judge," her mother said.

Prompted by his high viewpoint, Lesser drowsily recalled a performance he had once attended at a motel on the outskirts of a coastal city. Behind the bar in the cocktail lounge was a vast window that gave on a tank of illuminated water in which two perpetually smiling girls wearing fringed bathing suits did a routine, apparently in time to recorded tangos. The view from the window did not reveal either the surface or the bottom of the tank, so that at frequent intervals the swimmers would casually vanish into or reappear from vague and possibly illimitable regions. In the middle of the act, Lesser left the cocktail lounge and wandered through the motel grounds, which were planted with many kinds of succulents. He came at last to a small swimming pool. It was a cold night, and the pool steamed like one of the gulfs of Malebolge. Far below him, Lesser could see the swimmers silently engaged in their figures. He reflected that if he had first come upon them from this vantage, he would have thought they were in agony, and he considered how rarely we perceive a thing from more than one standpoint, and how often we are deluded.

Unexpectedly (for Lesser could not gauge the depth at which they evolved), the swimmers appeared among the vapors, where for a moment they floated exhausted. Lesser thought their expressions were forbearant, regretful, dispiteous. Then, acting on a signal the presence of which he was unaware, they dived, and Lesser felt, standing on the brink, peering into the luminous water in which they were descending and diminishing, how often he had found himself, an apprehensive spectator, poised above a writhing mystery.

Lesser fell asleep by the register, half of him on the linoleum, which was as rosy and speckled as a trout, half on the rug, which Grandma had braided during a severe winter. He was awakened by the effects of an electrical storm. It had roused the dogs and children, too; Lesser heard them going by his door and down the stairs. He looked through the grate and saw everybody huddled about the coffee table. Valerie's mother was cutting a strip off a palm frond with a sewing scissors. She laid the piece in an ashtray and lit it.

"What did you do that for, Grandma?" Lesser's stepson asked.

"To protect this house against the storm," she said. "It's blessed. Pray."

"I'll say an Our Father," Lesser's stepdaughter said. The faintly aromatic smoke rose through the register.

"Tell me about your father again," Lesser asked Valerie when she got into bed.

"What do you always want to hear that story for?" she said.

"Tell it to me," he said.

"You're a funny boy," she said. "One summer, when I was in the city of Paris—"

"What in the world were you doing there?"

"Oh, you know."

"Please tell it to me just once more."

"I was with young Eddie Quinlan, who always knew the latest dances."

"Were you in love with him?"

"Why not?"

"Then what happened?"

"My father stopped there on his way home from a visit to Italy. He had been where he was born and had bought the whole town meat and wine. They rang the church bells for him. He loved to be a big deal. He got into a cab at Orly and told the cabdriver who he was."

"The cabdriver didn't know him, did he?"

"Of course not. That was Pa's way. Somehow, he got him to understand that he was looking for his daughter but he had lost her address and he had no more money. He told the cabdriver he couldn't miss her, for she had red hair and blue eyes. They drove around Paris for hours and hours while my father looked for me out of one window, the cabdriver out of another. They never found me, so he took the next plane to New York."

"Where were you hiding?"

"In a room under the eaves on the sixth floor of the Hotel Félix, on the Rue Molière."

"What were you doing up there?"

"I was making love to Eddie Quinlan. When he got home, Pa mailed the fare to the cabdriver. He had given him his name and address."

"And a big tip, too."

"And a tremendous tip. Pa was a crazy tipper. People always did nice things for Pa. All he had to do was tell them who he was, which was nobody, of course."

"You didn't finish," Lesser said.

"Pa died before I could get home from Paris," she said.

"Do you think he would have found you if you hadn't been up there?"

"No," she said. "He told Ma before he died that after they had looked around for half an hour they got thirsty and sat down someplace and had a bunch of shots."

"That's a different ending," Lesser said.

"I knew you wouldn't like it, so I never told it to you before," she said. "It's like what you say about your awful detective stories—the ending never measures up to the beginning, and the mystery is always greater than the solution."

The following morning, Valerie said to Lesser, "I'm going to show you where I was born."

"I thought it was *here*," Lesser said in vain.

Grandma, her cousin, the children, and the dogs got in the back seat of the rented car; Valerie joined Lesser up front. After a ten minute drive, Lesser was told to turn off the Litchfield Road. At this point, Valerie said, "Ma, what's happened?"

"It's going on all over the place, dear," her mother said.

They were referring, Lesser gathered, to the dozen new ranch houses situated on one side of the secondary road; the houses were of more or less identical design, painted in several pastel colors, and undoubtedly "low-cost." The pavement ended at the last of them. Farther along, on the other side of the road, was Valerie's birthplace. It was a large, almost ruinous house with a screened porch, and lacking in any architectural distinction. A few severely blighted elms stood in the untended yard, heightening the predominant air of gloom and desuetude. Valerie told Lesser they had moved away when she was twelve, and that an old and reputedly eccentric spinster was the present tenant. It seemed to Lesser that the outing must have disappointed Valerie, for she had grown rather morose. He parked in front of the grim, inglorious house.

"All my children were born at home," Valerie's mother said. "Your wife was born right there." She pointed to a window on the second story; wisteria branched beneath the sill. As if her finger had been a conjurer's wand, a face that appeared to Lesser at first glance to be that of a little girl materialized in the window. This creature smiled and waved at them by fluttering in sequence the fingers of an otherwise immobile hand.

"There she is," Valerie's mother said.

"Isn't that a perfect shame," her cousin said.

Lesser then observed that her face was extensively

powdered, that what he had taken for girlish curls was, in fact, a cheap, ill-fitting wig, and that she was wearing a set of huge, dismaying false teeth. Valerie asked Lesser to drive on. Some yards beyond the house, where the road began to ascend a wooded hillside, a sign was posted:

ROAD OFFICIALLY CLOSED
PROCEED AT YOUR OWN RISK

Up ahead, the road deteriorated into little more than a wagon track. "When we went to school, we used to climb this road to where it meets the Guernseytown Road," Valerie said. "The school bus would stop there for us. Keep going."

"It's closed," Lesser said. "I'm not sure we'll be able to make it."

"Of course you can," Valerie said.

"I think we better go back," her son said.

"Valerie, we'll never in this world get up to the Guernseytown Road," her mother said. "The crews haven't been this way in ages."

"Howard can," Valerie said.

Lesser realized that, whether it was merely a whim or whether she had some deeper, ineffable purpose, Valerie was depending on him to drive them to the Guernseytown Road. He shifted into low. The road was sharply pitched, narrow, and had many turnings; in some places it was deeply rutted, in others it was partly washed out, revealing a number of smooth, pale boulders; it was murky throughout, because of the encroachment of the second growth.

"Please turn around, Howie," his stepdaughter said.

"We can't any more," Lesser said. The dogs began to whimper.

"I think you're both being very impetuous," Valerie's mother said. "We're going to get stuck in the middle of the woods, so help me God."

"I'm supposed to walk out of here in Cuban heels?" the cousin said. "Why doesn't anybody ever tell me anything anymore?"

"Valerie takes after her father," her mother said.

"I see," the cousin said.

"We're going to get lost," the boy said.

"Shut up," Lesser said.

In a few moments, they emerged on the Guernseytown Road. Valerie's mother said, "Clark Gable used to visit weekends with the people over there."

"Is that a fact," her cousin said.

Lesser felt that his marriage was not unlike, and as inexplicable as, the union of the shark and the remora, the bony fish that is the shark's inevitable companion, clinging unmolested to its belly by a suctorial disc, apparently contributing nothing to its welfare and feeding on the bits of food that fall from the shark's jaws while it eats. He, for this admittedly absurd apologue, would be the shark, Valerie the remora. He pictured them ineptly costumed, perhaps wearing pillowcases over their heads and feet; Valerie lying on her back beneath him, her arms about his waist; he sullenly dragging them both across the floor at a fancy-dress party, more as though they were the victims of a remote crash and he was trying to save her life than as faithful impersonators. When he bumped into someone, which happened fairly often, the rooms being crowded and his progress erratic and unsuspected, she would say, "*Excusez-moi*," and he would say, under his breath, "Why must you speak French?" As they regarded the other brilliant guests through ragged eyeholes, regretting that they had not come as something else, they would, from time to time, be asked by those who chanced to stumble across them—and who furthermore, understood that at their feet was a couple in meaningful disguise—what they were supposed to be. "The Shark and the Remora," Lesser would say hopefully, as if he were actually saying, "The Hare and the Tortoise," or "The Fox and the Grapes."

"I can't hear you with that thing on," would be the reply.

"I'm sorry," he would say, raising his voice. "We were unprepared."

He wished he could stand up, unmask, and explain the relationship. "You see," he would then say, "it's commensalism—dining at the same table—but the mystery is why she doesn't demand more than immunity from my ravages for the privilege of sharing my meals, and why I even tolerate these incursions."

Lesser had recounted these impressions to Valerie, pretending they had occurred in a dream. Valerie told him, "True. True. I see you forever wondering whether or not I'm getting away with anything, whether you're still intact, and if I *do* manage to get something from you, you feel you've been tragically diminished. Above all, you're so unwilling to be repaid. That is the saddest part. How dare you dream that dream!"

Lesser said, "If I have failed to please you, it isn't because I haven't tried."

Valerie said, "You always try to please me. 'Are you happy?' you say. 'Do you love me?' If you think I'm unhappy, you come over and kiss me—not because you want to kiss me but because you feel I need a kiss to be happy and that your duty is to insure my happiness. Like your father, you're a virtuous man. What you both want to see most of all is the imprint of your good works. If I'm smiling, then I'm happy. What you've done for me was all that was required to make me happy, so I'd better be smiling. You . . . you colonial!"

Lesser said, "You seem to forget that I married you, and that you're the only woman I ever married."

Valerie said, "You can't use this marriage as the answer to everything. It doesn't ultimately prove or demonstrate your love, you know. And another thing, you're so literal. If I say, for instance, 'I hate you,' you say, 'How can you hate me? I'm the nicest person you know.' "

"It's true," Lesser said. "I am."

"Then why don't you say, 'I want to make you happy' or, once in a while, 'I love you'? I'm always to understand how you feel without your ever expressing it. You're so precious with yourself. When I ask something of you in an emotional way, you move away—especially when you know that I'm asking it. You're most uncomfortable when I love you the most. Then there's no response. You seem to resent me, and that's something I hadn't bargained for."

"Let's play gin," Lesser said.

"However," Valerie went on, "I think your saving grace is that you know all these things yourself and accept the responsibility for them—not to change them necessarily but not to palm them off, either. I'm not sure your father has this perception. I hope you lose," she said, starting to shuffle the cards, "for it's in keeping with the way you think about yourself. You're such an ungracious winner."

When Lesser and Valerie returned to the city, a letter and a postcard awaited them. The letter was from Lesser's father; a pair of tickets to a Philharmonic concert were enclosed. "Dear Howard and Valerie," he had written, in the exceedingly legible hand that had changed little from the bygone time of the diaries, "Mother and I were the recipients of these seats, but (not so, alas) we have a United Cerebral Palsy function at the Americana the same evening. The program, Mother tells me, is chiefly Beethoven. To her chagrin, I don't attend concerts as frequently as in the past, since I find that my mind too readily wanders, and it was not, I am sure, Beethoven's intention to compose background music. I wonder if this is a symptom of my years. I don't entirely mean my inattention but rather this curious sense of moral responsibility with which I seem to be increasingly imbued. I must ask around among my contemporaries. As, no doubt, I have said more than once, there are not many of us left. Yesterday, walking back from the bank, I found myself, for some unaccountable reason, totting up all those whom I had known who had died during the past year. *Eheu fugaces*, etc. Love, Dad. P.S. Mother says these are '*good seats!*' "

The postcard was from the long-distance swimmer. She had returned to Hawaii, where Lesser had met her. She wrote that for the time being she was living on Queen Emma Square, next to a convent ("Ha! Ha!"), but would soon be moving to the twenty-fifth story of a new high-rise. "I've gotten a neat job with Pan Am," she concluded. "The surf is up. Don't be a stranger. XXX."

It was obvious, Lesser thought, that she hadn't heard

of his marriage. He recalled how she always looked in sleep—one leg drawn up so that the knee was nearly level with her breasts, a position that suggested she was trying to scale a wall, to escape but—from what? Her dreams? This world? Her reference to the surf brought to mind a photograph she had once shown him of herself riding on a twenty-foot wave at Makaha. It was somewhat out of focus, being made from a frame of movie film. A moment after it was taken, she went, as she had said, laughing, "down the tubes." Striving to reach the surface in the almost unstaining mixture of air and water that was the wake of the broken wave, she came instead to the bottom. Another surfer, paddling out, found her, unconscious. "He saw my hair floating," she said. "I was wearing it very long that year."

Lesser listened to his stepchildren, who were, he knew, kneeling together at the vaporous tub, bathing the dogs and singing to them; the mirrors would be covered with their cabalistic signs. "We are the joy boys of radio—hello, hello, hello, hello," they sang. It was an old number he had taught them—at least, as much of it as he had remembered. He wondered whether the swimmer's plight in the white water, her survival, was at all a lesson that could be applied to life at large, and if to any extent it was reversible, in the sense that if one thought he was steadily approaching the bottom he might at last, in his prodigious ignorance, be coming up for air.

" 'Nani Li'i Natural Color Card,' " Valerie read from the postcard. " 'Say "Nonnie Le'e,' " it's Hawaiian for "Little Beauty." ' " Lesser gathered she had been standing behind him for some time.

"What's wrong?" he said at length. "That's all I seem to be saying these days, isn't it?"

"The same thing as last week, and the week before that," she said. "The only thing that's different is that time passes."

He felt her hand on his shoulder. They were, he realized, in the attitude of Dante and Vergil in so many of Doré's illustrations—overlooking abysses, on vile, desolate slopes, or crossing great sheets of ice; one fearful and astonished, the other serene.

At the Tepid Baths

I am sojourning in a city in the South, the veritable South upon which shines the radiance of the quadruple star. The city rises, bleakly at this season, from both sides of an ancient river bed along which the principal street, Queen Street, is laid out. In one direction, it ascends, crossing the Karangahape Road—the intersection where Ealey said he had such difficulty catching the bus—before petering out; in the other, it descends to the wharfs. In the evening, I often go down to Queen Street and walk beneath the verandas with the crowds. It is winter here and rains a good deal of the time. I have found moss and some small weeds growing on the sidewalk in the heart of the city. By and large, I am dismayed and disappointed by what I see of my fellow man, his works.

I am staying at the Hotel de l'Isle on Albert Street. "It has quite superior amenities, and the tariff's most reasonable, don't you think?" Ealey had said at the Tepid Baths. "How do you find the dining room? A bit Frenchy?" I said it suited me. "Very pink," Ealey said. "Those little birds are rather fanciful, though, aren't they? I've noticed that no one ever cuts their little toenails. Really shocking, in a way." Recessed into one of the walls of the dining room are two great gilded cages containing a number of Java temple birds. The backs of the cages are mirrored, which not only enhances their size but gives the occasionally disconcerting illusion of there being twice as many birds as there really are. The de l'Isle abounds in mirrors. For instance, there is one at the end of my corridor—huge, inexplicably situated, and distorting, and it serves to confirm my sense of futility and imperfection. "Have you taken a real look at the service?" Ealey had said. "Go ahead and turn it over next time. Says 'Super-Vitrified' right there. That's quality." I told him I hadn't noticed. "Got much of a view?" Ealey asked. I said I had hardly any. "Yes, not very scenic, the prospect from the de l'Isle, actually," he said. Across the way is the La Danza Coffee Shop, and four stories above it there are some rooms that must be a sort of a club, for most nights middle-aged couples dance by the windows singing "Goody Goody" to each other.

I met Ealey at the Tepid Baths, the salt-water pool at the foot of Hobson Street. It was one of those chance encounters such as take place in railway waiting rooms, which customarily turn out to have a faintly moral and melancholy tone. The Tepid Baths! Lofty, dim, dinned, steaming, Pompeian. Vague forms writhe and shout in its vapors. Viennese waltzes blare from loudspeakers. Coaches with the look of greyhound trainers—little, dusky, Brythonic men with caps and coat sweaters under their jackets—pace up and down on the dank tiles, cooing to their swimmers. Stopwatches hang on shoelaces about their necks. At night, TEPID BATHS burns in red neon on its tall smokestack.

Ealey was at the shallow end, almost entirely immersed, wearing a rented suit. He is past fifty, immensely pale, and his mustache extends on to his cheeks. "How do you do?" he said. He held out his hand as though he had little expectation of it being taken. Around his wrist was the elastic band to which his locker key was attached. "Ealey's my name," he said. He did a brief, extraordinary imitation of a belly dancer. It was obviously something he had often practiced. "Wriggly," he explained. "Like an eel, but spelled differently. First 'e' is the same, but then you have an 'a.' Underhand, that one, I expect. Most people fall down there. *Nota bene*. Following that 'a' is an 'l,' naturally.

Then we have the second 'e,' another trouble spot, you see. Bringing up the rear is a 'y.' Spells Ealey, doesn't it." He seemed distressed by this inevitable conclusion. "I'm in the public-relations end of things," he added, improbably. I excused myself and swam to the far end. The water was undeniably tepid and rank, as though it had been pumped from the bottom of the harbor. "I was watching you," Ealey said when I returned. "Pretty stroke you've got there. Sound wind, too, I suppose. I've never got the hang of the Australian crawl, myself, but I enjoy soaking these bones here for the odd half hour, whenever I can get away." For some reason, it was hard to picture Ealey as a vertebrate. "I'm convenient," he continued. "Next to the Britomart Car Park." He appeared to be fascinated by my hair. "You'd do well to let me introduce you to my hairdresser," he said at length. "He's got a first-class location on Khartoum Place." He then asked me where I was staying, and we talked about the de l'Isle for a while. The idea that I didn't have much of a view disturbed him disproportionately. Oppressed by his gloomy, prosaic revelations, his despair, I made to leave. "An out-of-the-way thing happened to me day before yesterday," he said, beginning an interminable account of his experience with the No. 6 bus; he might have been describing an early-nineteenth-century battle. I swam off during one of his great pauses, never learning whether he finally caught it.

The steam seemed to be more profuse. Brutish, indefinite figures loomed, swerved, dived, disappeared. A hand lay briefly on me. In the next lane, I descried a girl going by, doing the backstroke, and regarding, with parted lips, the distant ceiling, which was adorned with vast, pagan revels ineptly executed in distemper. I pursued her. She was no more than twelve, the age of my stepdaughter, and no less beautiful. She had touched me with charm, grace, and inadvertence. Swimming on her other side was a scowling man. Once in a while, he corrected her stroke in a particularly harsh voice. We went up and back together. Ealey was waiting for me at the shallow end, looking like some seedy, retributive sea god. "He gave you the fishy eye," he told me. I said I didn't know what he was talking about. "Her father," Ealey said. "He's training her to be a champion. I wouldn't interfere there. He's very fit." I told Ealey he was mistaken. "What's your game, actually?" he asked. I said that, among other things, my wife misrepresented me in her dreams, that as my stepchildren became older they lost the illusion of anonymity and grew more and more to resemble their father, that my brother believed I had betrayed him, that my dogs cowered beneath the couch when I came home, and that I was a plagiarist. There was an announcement over the loudspeakers that the baths were closing. Men in rubber boots stood impatiently about the edges with long-handled brushes. The swimmers were leaving, slowly climbing out of the misty pool as though reënacting their ancestral sorrow.

I was about to follow when I was arrested by someone singing.

" '*Ich grol-le nicht, und wenn das Herz—auch bricht.*
E-wig ver-lor'-nes Lieb, e-wig ver-lor'-nes Lieb . . .' "

It was Ealey, the water up to his waist, his voice, unexpectedly, *basso cantante*, fervent, and ennobling.

" '*Ich sah dich ja im Trau-me*
Und sah die Nacht in dei-nes Her-zens Rau-me,
Und sah die Schlang; die dir am Her-zen frisst, —
Ich sah, mein Lieb, wie sehr du e-lend bist . . .' "

He broke off. "Before you were born it was my ambition to go on the concert stage," he said. Had I been, once more, deluded and derided? "You're in good voice tonight, Mr. Ealey," said one of the men with the brushes.

The Fencing Master

I live above a fencing academy. It is on the second floor, I am on the third. At first, I couldn't sleep because of the great, alien din which persisted far into the night: clashing weapons, footfalls, the fencing master's splendid and energetic cries: "*Et la. La. La. La.*" Now I am disturbed because for the past few days it has been silent beneath me. Has something happened to the master or his pupils?

I go downstairs and knock at his door. In a moment it is opened by a figure wearing a fencing costume and mask.

"Are you the fencing master?" I ask.

"I am," he says and shows me in.

Although I have often seen his pupils on the stairs, this is the first I have got a look at him. His *salle d'armes*, which was formerly a ballroom, and, I have heard, serves as his apartment as well, is bare, save for three linoleum *pistes*, and very poorly lit. The walls are covered with damask, cherubim and seraphim look down from the ceiling, and several dead, weightless wasps lie along the baseboards.

"I live above you," I say. "I was concerned because I have not been hearing you giving your lessons."

"My pupils have left me," he says.

"Every one?"

"Fencing has gone out of fashion," he says.

"What will you do then?"

"What can I do? I am a fencing master. My father was a fencing master. His father was a fencing master. We have always been fencing masters in my family. My father told me that one day fencing would no longer be in fashion. His father told him the same. It is our fate."

"Why didn't you make provision then?"

"To be a fencing master one must devote every minute of one's life to fencing," he says. "Like all arts, it can always be perfected. The least amount of time spent in another direction can never be recovered, and one is perpetually the lesser fencer for it. Of course, one needs an opponent. What a marvellous thing it would be if one could learn to fence by oneself."

As though he regards the act of putting on his mask a waste of time, he has not removed it. Does he never take it off? I picture him pacing beneath me, waiting in vain for another fencer to appear. He cannot leave or he might irrevocably miss the arrival of the last ignorant fencer. If he sleeps, it must be only for a few minutes, curled on a *piste*, fully costumed, ready to spring into action.

Several days later, I meet three young men in the street whom I recognize as having been among the fencing master's old pupils. I introduce myself and tell them of my visit.

"He was a good teacher, but now he is too old and feeble," says one.

"Do you know that he is blind?" says another. "He won't admit it. He is very proud."

"Actually, he is mad," says the third. "How can you tell a person such a thing?"

"You see why we had to leave him," says the first. "He will not face up to the truth. What could we tell him but that fencing has gone out of fashion? We have all enrolled at another academy. The master is first-class."

I must move, I must move. How can I continue to live here with the knowledge that he is writhing below me? The only way I can help is to take fencing lessons from him, but that would occupy too much of my time, and, besides, I'm sure I would never excel. I must move. Why do I have to be the one to find him lying among the carcasses of the wasps?

About the Author

GILBERT ROGIN was born in 1929 in New York. He attended the State University of Iowa and is a graduate of Columbia College. He was first published in *discovery* in 1955, and his stories have since appeared in *The New Yorker*, *Vogue*, *Esquire* and *Mademoiselle*. He is married and lives in New York City.